THE VERY SMALL PERSON

BY

ANNIE HAMILTON DONNELL

The Very Small Person

Chapter I

Little Blue Overalls

Miss Salome's face was gently frowning as she wrote.

"Dear John," the letter began,—"It's all very well except one thing. I wonder you didn't think of that. I'm thinking of it most of the time, and it takes away so much of the pleasure of the rose-garden and the raspberry-bushes! Anne is in raptures over the raspberry-bushes.

"Yes, the raspberries and the roses are all right. And I like the stone-wall with the woodbine over it. (Good boy, you remembered that, didn't you?) And the apple-tree and the horse-chestnut and the elm—of course I like them.

"The house is just big enough and just small enough, and there's a trunk-closet, as I stipulated. And Anne's room has a 'southern exposure'—Anne's crazy spot is southern exposures. Mine's it. Dear, dear, John, how could you forget it! That everything else—closets and stone-walls and exposures—should be to my mind but that! Well, I am thinking of moving out, before I move in. But I haven't told Anne. Anne is the kind of person not to tell, until the last moment. It saves one's nerves—heigh-ho! I thought I was coming here to get away from nerves! I was so satisfied. I really meant to thank you, John, until I discovered—it. Oh yes, I know—Elizabeth is looking over your shoulder, and you two are saying something that is unfit for publication about old maids! My children, then thank the Lord you aren't either of you old maids. Make the most of it."

Miss Salome let her pen slip to the bare floor and gazed before her wistfully. The room was in the dreary early stages of unpacking, but it was not of that Miss Salome was thinking. Her eyes were gazing out of the window at a thin gray trail of smoke against the blue ground of the sky. She could see the little house, too, brown and tiny and a little battered. She could see the clothes-line, and count easily enough the pairs of little stockings on it. She caught up the pen again fiercely.

"There are eight," she wrote. "Allowing two legs to a child, doesn't that make four? John Dearborn, you have bought me a house next door to four children! I think I shall begin to put the books back to-night. As ill luck will have it, they are all unpacked.

"I have said nothing to Anne; Anne has said nothing to me. But we both know. She has counted the stockings too. We are both old maids. No, I have not seen them yet—anything but their stockings on the clothes-line. But the mother is not a washer-woman—there is no hope. I don't know how I know she isn't a washer-woman, but I do. It is impressed upon me. So there are four children, to say nothing of the Lord knows how many babies still in socks! I cannot forgive you, John."

Miss Salome had been abroad for many years. Stricken suddenly with homesickness, she and her ancient serving-woman, Anne, had fled across seas to their native land. Miss Salome had first commissioned John, long-suffering John,—adviser, business-manager, brother,—to find her a snug little home with specified adjuncts of trunk-closets, elm, apple, and horse-chestnut trees, woodbiney stone walls—and a "southern exposure" for Anne. John had done his best. But how could he have forgotten, and Elizabeth have forgotten, and Miss Salome herself have forgotten—it? Every one knew Miss Salome's distaste for little children. Anne's too, though Anne was more taciturn than her mistress.

"Hullo!"

Miss Salome started. In the doorway stood a very small person in blue jeans overalls.

"Hullo! I want your money or your life! I'm a 'wayman."

"A—what?" Miss Salome managed to ejaculate. The Little Blue Overalls advanced a few feet into the room.

"Robber, you know;—you know what robbers are, don't you? I'm one. You needn't call me a highwayman, I'm so—so low. Just 'wayman 'll do. Why, gracious! you ain't afraid, are you? You needn't be,—I won't hurt you!" and a sweet-toned, delighted little laugh echoed through the bare room. "You needn't give me your money or your life. Never mind. I'll 'scuse you."

Miss Salome uttered no word at all. Of course this boy belonged in a pair of those stockings over there. It was no more than was to be expected.

"It's me. I'm not a 'wayman any more,—just me. I heard you'd come, so I thought I'd come an' see you. You glad? Why don't you ask me will I take a seat?"

"Will I—will you take a seat?" repeated Miss Salome, as if she were saying a lesson. The Little Blue Overalls climbed into a chair.

"Looks pretty bad here, doesn't it? I guess you forgot to sweep," he said, assuming social curves in his plump little body. He had the air of having come to stay. Miss Salome's lips, under orders to tighten, found themselves unexpectedly relaxing into a smile. The Little Blue Overalls was amusing.

"We've got a sofy, an' a rockin'-chair. The sofy's new, but Chessie's broke a hole in it."

"Are there four of you?" Miss Salome asked, abruptly. It was the Little Blue Overalls' turn to start now.

"Me?—gracious! four o' me? I guess you're out o' your head, aren't— Oh, you mean child'en! Well, there's five, 'thout countin' the spandy new one—she's too little to count."

Five—six, with the spandy new one! Miss Salome's gaze wandered from the piles of books on the floor to the empty packing-boxes, as if trying to find the shortest distance.

"There are only four pairs on the line," she murmured, weakly,—"stockings," she added. The Little Blue Overalls nodded comprehendingly.

"I don't wear 'em summers,—I guess you didn't notice I was in my bare feet, did you? Well, I am. It's a savin'. The rest are nothing but girls—I'm all the boy we've got. Boys are tough. But I don't s'pose you ever was one, so you don't know?" There was an upward inflection to the voice of the Little Blue Overalls. An answer seemed expected.

"No—no, I never was one," Miss Salome said, hastily. She could hear Anne's plodding steps in the hall. It would be embarrassing to have Anne come in now. But the footsteps plodded by. After more conversation on a surprising number of topics, the Little Blue Overalls climbed out of the chair.

"I've had a 'joyable time, an' I'll be pleased to come again, thank you," he said, with cheerful politeness. "I'm glad you've come,—I like you, but I hope you'll sweep your floor." He retreated a few steps, then faced about again and advanced into the enemy's near neighborhood. He was holding out a very small, brown, unwashed hand. "I forgot 'bout shakin' hands," he smiled. "Le's. I hope you like me, too, an' I guess you do, don't you? Everybody does. Nobody ever didn't like me in my life, an' I'm seven. Good-bye."

Miss Salome heard him patter down the hall, and she half thought—she was not sure—that at the kitchen door he stopped. Half an hour afterwards she saw a very small person crossing the rose-garden. If there was something in his hands that he was eating, Miss Salome never asked Anne about it. It was not her way to ask Anne questions. It was not Anne's way to ask her. The letter to John was finished, oddly enough, without further mention of—it. Miss Salome got the broom and swept the bare big room carefully. She hummed a little as she worked. Out in the kitchen Anne was humming too.

"It is a pleasant little place, especially the stone-wall and the woodbine," Miss Salome was thinking; "I'm glad I specified woodbine and stone-walls. John would never have thought. So many other things are pleasant, too; but, dear, dear, it is very unfortunate about that one thing!" Still Miss Salome hummed, and after tea she got Anne to help her move out the empty packing-boxes.

The next day the Little Blue Overalls came again. This time he was a peddler, with horse-chestnut "apples" to sell, and rose-petal pies. He said they were bargains.

"You can truly eat the pies," he remarked. "There's a little sugar in 'em. I saved it off the top o' her bun," indicating Anne's locality with a jerk of his little cropped head. So it was a fact, was it? He had been eating something when he crossed the rose-garden? Miss Salome wondered at Anne.

The next day, and the next,—every day the Little Blue Overalls came, always in a new character. Miss Salome found herself watching for him. She could catch the little blue glint of very small overalls as soon as they got to the far side of the rose-garden. But for Anne, at the end of the first week she would have gone out to meet him. Dear, dear, but for Miss Salome, Anne would have gone!

The Little Blue Overalls confided his troubles to Miss Salome. He told her how hard it was to be the only boy,—how impossible, of course, it was to play girly plays, and how he had longed to find a congenial spirit. Mysteriously enough, he appeared confident that he had found the congenial spirit at last. Miss Salome's petticoats seemed no obstacle. He showed her his pocketful of treasures. He taught her to whittle, and how to bear it when she "bleeded." He taught her to whistle—very softly, on account of Anne. (He taught Anne, too—softly, on account of Miss Salome.) He let her make sails for his boats, and sew on his buttons,—those that Anne didn't sew on.

"Dear John," wrote Miss Salome, "the raspberries are ripe. When you were a very small person—say seven—did you ever mash them between raspberry leaves, with 'sugar in,' and call them pies,—and eat them? They are really palatable. Of course it is a little risky on account of possible bugs. I don't remember that you were a remarkable little boy. Were you? Did you ever play you were a highwayman, or an elephant, or anything of that sort? Queer I can't remember.

"Anne is delighted with her southern exposure, but she has never said so. That is why I know she is. I am delighted with the roses and the closets and the horse-chestnut—especially the horst-chestnut. That is where we play—I mean it is most pleasant there, hot afternoons. Did you use to dote on horse-chestnuts? Queer boys should. But I rather like them myself, in a way,—out of the way! We have picked up a hundred and seventeen." Miss Salome dropped into the plural number innocently, and Elizabeth laughed over John's shoulder. Elizabeth did the reading between the lines. John was only a man.

One day Little Blue Overalls was late. He came from the direction of the stable that adjoined Miss Salome's house. He was excited and breathless. A fur rug was draped around his shoulders and trailed uncomfortably behind him.

"Come on!" he cried, eagerly. "It's a circus! I'm the grizzled bear. There's a four-legged girl—Chessie, you know, with stockin's on her hands,—and a Manx rooster ('thout any tail), and, oh, my! the splendidest livin' skeleton you ever saw! I want you to be man'ger—come on! It's easy enough. You poke us with a stick, an' we perform. I dance, an' the four-legged girl walks, an' the rooster crows, an' the skeleton skel— Oh, well, you needn't poke the skeleton."

The Little Blue Overalls paused for breath. Miss Salome laid aside her work. Where was Anne?—but the stable could be reached without passing the kitchen windows. Saturdays Anne was very busy, anyway.

"I'm ready," laughed Miss Salome. She had never been a circus-manager, but she could learn. It was easier than whittling. Together they hurried away to the stable. At the door Miss Salome came to an abrupt stop. An astonished exclamation escaped her.

The living skeleton sat on an empty barrel, lean and grave and patient. The living skeleton also uttered an exclamation. She and the circus-manager gazed at each other in a remarkable way, as if under a spell.

"Come on!" shouted the grizzled bear.

After that, Miss Salome and Anne were not so reserved. What was the use? And it was much easier, after all, to be found out. Things ran along smoothly and pleasantly after that.

Late in the autumn, Elizabeth, looking over John's shoulder one day, laughed, then cried out, sharply. "Oh!" she said; "oh, I am sorry!" And John echoed her an instant later.

"Dear John," the letter said, "when you were little were you ever very sick, and did you die? Oh, I see, but don't laugh. I think I am a little out of my head to-day. One is when one is anxious. And Little Blue Overalls is very sick. I found Anne crying a little while ago, and just now she came in and found me. She didn't mind; I don't.

"He did not come yesterday or the day before. Yesterday I went to see why. Anne was just coming away from the door. 'He's sick,' she said, in her crisp, sharp way,—you know it, John,—but she was white in the face. The little mother came to the door. Queer I had never seen her before,—Little Blue Overalls has her blue eyes.

"There were two or three small persons clinging to her, and the very smallest one I ever saw was in her arms. She looked fright—" The letter broke off abruptly here. Another slip was enclosed that began as abruptly. "Anne says it is scarlet-fever. The doctor has been there just now. I am going to have him brought over here—you know I don't mean the doctor. And you would not smile, either of you—not Elizabeth, anyway, for she will think of her own babies—"

"Yes, yes," Elizabeth cried, "I am thinking!"

"—That is why he must not stay over there. There are so many babies. I am going over there now."

The letter that followed this one was a week delayed.

"Dear John," it said,—"you must be looking out for another place. If anything should—he is very sick, John! And I could not stay here without him. Nor Anne. John, would you ever think that Anne was born a nurse? Well, the Lord made her one. I have found it out. Not with a little dainty white cap on, and a nurse's apron,—not that kind, but with light, cool fingers and a great, tender heart. That is the Lord's kind, and it's Anne. She is taking beautiful care of our Little Blue Overalls. The little mother and I appreciate Anne. But he is very very sick, John.

"I could not stay here. Why, there isn't a spot that wouldn't remind me! There's a faint little path worn in the grass beside the stone-wall where he has been 'sentry.' There's a bare spot under the horse-chestnut where he played blacksmith and 'shoe-ed' the saw-horse. And he used to pounce out on me from behind the old elm and demand my money or my life,—he was a highwayman the first time I saw him. I've bought rose-pies and horse-chestnut apples of him on the front door-steps. We've played circus in the barn. We've been Indians and gypsies and Rough Riders all over the place. You must look round for another one, John. I can't stay here.

"Here's Anne. She says he is asleep now. Before he went he sent word to me that he was a wounded soldier, and he wished I'd make a red cross and sew it on Anne's sleeve. I must go and make it. Good-bye. The letter will not smell good because I shall fumigate it, on account of Elizabeth's babies. You need not be afraid."

There was no letter at all the next week, early or late, and they were afraid Little Blue Overalls was dead. Elizabeth hugged her babies close and cried softly over their little, bright heads. Then shortly afterwards the telegram came, and she laughed—and cried—over that. It was as welcome as it was guiltless of punctuation:

"Thank the Lord John Little Blue Overalls is going to get well."

Chapter II
The Boy

The trail of the Boy was always entirely distinct, but on this especial morning it lay over house, porch, barn—everything. The Mother followed it up, stooping to gather the miscellany of boyish belongings into her apron. She had a delightful scheme in her mind for clearing everything up. She wanted to see how it would seem, for once, not to have any litter of whittlings, of strings and marbles and tops! No litter of beloved birds' eggs, snake-skins, turtle-shells! No trail of the Boy anywhere.

It had taken the whole family to get the Boy off, but now he was gone. Even yet the haze of dust the stage-coach had stirred up from the dry roadway lingered like a faint blur on the landscape. It could not be ten minutes since they had bidden the Boy his first good-bye. The Mother smiled softly.

"But I did it!" she murmured. "Of course,—I had to. The idea of letting your Boy go off without kissing him good-bye! Mary," she suddenly spoke aloud, addressing the Patient Aunt, who was following the trail too, picking up the siftings from the other's apron—"Mary, did you kiss him? There was really no need, you know, because you are not his mother. And it would have saved his feelings not to."

The Patient Aunt laughed. She was very young and pretty, and the "patient" in her name had to do only with her manner of bearing the Boy.

"No, I didn't," she said. "I didn't dare to, after I saw him wipe yours off!"

"Mary!"

"With the back of his hand. I am not near-sighted. Now why should a well-meaning little kiss distress a Boy like that? That's what I want to know."

"It didn't once," sighed the Mother, gently. "Not when he was a baby. I'm glad I got in a great many of them then, while I had a chance. It was the trousers that did it, Mary. From the minute he put on trousers he objected to being kissed. I put his kilts on again one day, and he let me kiss him."

"But it was a bribe to get you to take them off," laughed the Patient Aunt, wickedly. "I remember;—I was there. And you took them off to pay for that kiss. You can't deny it, Bess."

"Yes, I took them off—and after that I kissed them. It was next best. Mary, does it seem very awful quiet here to you?"

"Awful. I never heard anything like it in my life. I'm going to let something drop and make a noise." She dropped a tin trumpet, but it fell on the thick rug, and they scarcely heard it.

The front gate clicked softly, and the Father came striding up the walk, whistling exaggeratedly. He had ridden down to the corner with the Boy.

"Well, well, well," he said; "now I shall go to work. I'm going up to my den, girls, and I don't want to be called away for anything or anybody lower than a President or the minister. This is my first good chance to work for ten years."

Which showed how old the Boy was. He was rather young to go off alone on a journey, but a neighbor half a mile down the glary white road was going his way, and would take him in charge. The neighbor was lame, and the Boy thought he was going to take charge of the neighbor. It was as well. Nobody had undeceived him.

In a little over half an hour—three-quarters at most—the trail of the Boy was wiped out. Then the Patient Aunt and the Mother sat down peacefully and undisturbed to their sewing. Everything was very spruce and cleared up. The Mother was thinking of that, and of how very, very still it was. She wished the Patient Aunt would begin to sing, or a door would slam somewhere.

"Dear me!" she thought, with a tremulous little smile, "here I am wanting to hear a door slam already! Any one wouldn't think I'd had a special set of door nerves for years!" She started in to rock briskly. There used to be a board that creaked by the west window. Why didn't it creak now? The Mother tried to make it.

"Mary," she cried, suddenly and sharply—"Mary!"

"Mercy! Well, what is it, my dear? Is the house afire, or anything?"

"Why don't you talk, and not sit there as still as a post? You haven't said a word for half an hour."

"Why, so I haven't,—or you either, for that matter. I thought we were sitting here enjoying the calm. Doesn't it look too lovely and fixed-up for anything, Bess? Seems like Sunday. Don't you wish somebody would call before we get stirred up again?"

"There's time enough. We sha'n't get stirred up again for a week," sighed the Mother. She seemed suddenly to remember, as a new thing, that weeks held seven days apiece; days, twenty-four hours. The little old table at school repeated itself to her mind. Then she remembered how the Boy said it. She saw him toeing the stripe in the carpet before her; she heard his high sweet sing-song:

"Sixty sec-unds make a min-it. Sixty min-its make a nour. Sixty hours make—no; I mean twenty-four hours—make a d-a-a-y."

That was the way the Boy said it—God bless the Boy! The Mother got up abruptly.

"I think I will go up and call on William," she said, unsteadily. The Patient Aunt nodded gravely. "But he doesn't like to be interrupted, you know," she reminded, thinking of the Boy's interruptions.

Up-stairs, the Father said "Come in," with remarkable alacrity. He looked up from his manuscripts and welcomed her. The sheets, tossed untidily about the table were mostly blank ones.

"Well, dear?" the little Mother said, with a question in her voice.

"Not at all;—bad," he answered, gloomily. "I haven't written a word yet, Bess. At this rate, how soon will my new book be out? It's so confoundedly still—"

"Yes, dear, I know," the Mother said, hastily. Then they both gazed out of the window, and saw the Boy's little, rough-coated, ugly dog moping under the Boy's best-beloved tree. The Boy had pleaded hard to be allowed to take the dog on the journey. They both remembered that now.

"He's lonesome," murmured the Mother, but she meant that they two were. And they had thought it would be such a rest and relief! But then, you remember, the Boy had never been away before, and he was only ten.

So one day and one more after it dragged by. Two from seven leaves five. The Mother secretly despaired. The second night, after the others were asleep, she stole around the house and strewed the Boy's things about in all the rooms; but she could not make them look at ease. Nevertheless, she let them lie, and, oddly enough, no one appeared to see them next morning. All the family made fine pretence of being cheerful, and spoke often of the quietude and peace—how restful it was; how they had known beforehand that it would be so, without the whooping, whistling, tramping, slamming Boy.

"So relieving to the nerves," the Patient Aunt said.

"So soothing," murmured the Mother, sadly.

"So confoundedly nice and still!" the Father muttered in his beard. "Haven't had such a chance to work for ten years." But he did not work. The third day he said he must take a little run to the city to—to see his publishers, you know. There were things that needed looking after;—if the Mother would toss a few things into his grip, he'd be off;—back in a few days, of course. And so he went. It was a relief to the Mother, and a still further one when, on the fourth day, the Patient Aunt went away on a little visit to—to some friends.

"I'm glad they're gone," nodded the little Mother, decisively, "for I couldn't have stood it another day—not another day! Now I'm going away myself. I suppose I should have gone anyway, but it's much pleasanter not to have them know. They would both of them have laughed. What do they know about being a Mother and having your little Boy away? Oh yes, they can laugh and be relieved—and rested—and soothed! It's mothers whose hearts break with lonesomeness—mothers and ugly little dogs." She took the moping little beast up in her lap and stroked his rough coat.

"You shall go too," she whispered. "You can't wait three days more, either, can you? It would have killed you, too, wouldn't it? We are glad those other people went away, aren't we? Now we'll go to the Boy."

Early the next morning they went. The Mother thought she had never been so happy before in her life, and the ugly little beast yelped with anticipative joy. In a little—a very little—while, now, they would hear the Boy shout—see him caper—feel his hard little palms on their faces. They would see the trail of the Boy over everything; not a make-believe, made-up trail, but the real, littered, Boy thing.

"I hope those other two people are enjoying their trips. We are, aren't we?" cried the happy Mother, hugging the little ugly dog in her arms. "And they won't know;—they can't laugh at us. We'll never let them know we couldn't bear it another minute, will we? The Boy sha'n't tell on us."

The place where the Boy was visiting was quite a long way from the railroad station, but they trudged to it gayly, jubilantly. While yet a good way off they heard the Boy and came upon his trail. The little dog nearly went into fits with frantic joy at the cap he found in the path, but the Mother went straight on to meet the little shouting voice in her ears. Half-way to it she saw the Boy. But wait. Who was that with him? And that other one, laughing in his beard? If there had been time to be surprised—but she only brushed them both aside and caught up the Boy. The Boy—the Boy—the Boy again! She kissed him all over his freckled, round little face. She kissed his hair and his hands and his knees.

"Look out; he's wiping them off!" laughed the Patient Aunt. "But you see he didn't wipe mine off."

"You didn't kiss me. You darsn't. You ain't my mother," panted the Boy, between the kisses. He could not keep up with them with the back of his brown little hand.

"But I am, dear. I'm your mother," cooed the Mother, proud of herself.

After a while she let him go because she pitied him. Then she stood up, stern and straight, and demanded things of these other two.

"How came you here, Mary? I thought you were going on a visit. Is this the way you see your publishers, William?"

"I—I couldn't wait," murmured the Impatient Aunt. "I wanted to hear him shout. You know how that is, Bess." But there was no apology in the Father's tone. He put out his hand and caught the Boy as he darted past, and squared him about, with his sturdy little front to his mother. The Father was smiling in a tender way.

"He is my publisher," he said. "I would rather he published my best works than any one else. He will pay the highest royalty."

And the Mother, when she slipped across to them, kissed not the Boy alone, but them both.

The next day they took the Boy back in triumph, the three of them and the little dog, and after that there was litter and noise and joy as of old.

Chapter III
The Adopted

The Enemy's chin just reached comfortably to the top fence-rail, and there it rested, while above it peered a pair of round blue eyes. It is not usual for an enemy's eyes to be so round and blue, nor an enemy's chin to reach so short a distance from the ground.

"She's watching me," Margaret thought; "she wants to see if I've got far as she has. 'Fore I'd lean my chin on folks's gates and watch 'em!"

"She knows I'm here," reflected the Enemy, "just as well as anything. 'Fore I'd peek at people out o' the ends o' my eyes!"

Between the two, a little higher than their heads, tilted a motherly bird on a syringa twig.

"Ter-wit, ter-wee,—pit-ee, pit-ee!" she twittered under her breath. And it did seem a pity to be quarrellers on a day in May, with the apple buds turning as pink as pink!

"I sha'n't ever tell her any more secrets," Margaret mused, rather sadly, for there was that beautiful new one aching to be told.

"I sha'n't ever skip with her again," the Enemy's musings ran drearily, and the arm she had always put round Margaret when they skipped felt lonesome and—and empty. And there was that lovely new level place to skip in!

"Pit-ee! Pit-ee!" sang softly the motherly bird.

It had only been going on a week of seven days. It was exactly a week ago to-day it began, while they were making the birthday presents together, Margaret sitting in this very chair and Nell—the Enemy sitting on the toppest door-step. Who would have thought it was coming? There was nothing to warn—no thunder in the sky, no little mother-bird on the syringa bush. It just came—oh, hum!

"I'm ahead!" the Enemy had suddenly announced, waving her book-mark. She had got to the "h" in her Mother, and Margaret was only finishingher capital "M." They were both working "Honor thy Mother that thy days may be long," on strips of cardboard for their mothers' birthdays, which, oddly enough, came very close together. Of course that wasn't exactly the way it was in the Bible, but they had agreed it was better to leave "thy Father" out because it wasn't his birthday, and they had left out "the land which the Lord thy God giveth" because there wasn't room for it on the cardboard.

"I'm ahead!"

"That's because I'm doing mine the carefulest," Margaret had retorted, promptly. "There aren't near so many hunchy places in mine."

"Well, I don't care; my mother's the best-looking, if her book-mark isn't!" in triumph. "Her hair curls, and she doesn't have to wear glasses."

Margaret's wrath had flamed up hotly. Mother's eyes were so shiny and tender behind the glasses, and her smooth brown hair was so soft! The love in Margaret's soul arose and took up arms for Mother.

"I love mine the best, so there!—so there!—so there!" she cried. But side by side with the love in her soul was the secret consciousness of how very much the Enemy loved her mother, too. Now, sitting sewing all alone, with the Enemy on the other side of the fence, Margaret knew she had not spoken truly then, but the rankling taunt of the curls that Mother hadn't, and the glasses that she had, justified her to herself. She would never, never take it back, so there!—so there!—so there!

"She's only got to the end o' her 'days,'—I can see clear from here," soliloquized the Enemy, with awakening exultation. For the Enemy's "days" were "long,"—she had finished her book-mark. The longing to shout it out—"I've got mine done!"—was so intense within her that her chin lost its balance on the fence-rail and she jarred down heavily on her heels. So close related are mind and matter.

Margaret resorted to philosophic contemplation to shut out the memory of the silent onlooker at the fence. She had swung about discourteously "back to" her. "I guess," contemplated Margaret, "my days 'll be long enough in the land! I guess so, for I honor my mother enough to live forever! That makes me think—I guess I better go in and kiss her good-night for to-night when she won't be at home."

It was mid-May and school was nearly over. The long summer vacation stretched endlessly, lonesomely, ahead of Margaret. Last summer it had been so different. A summer vacation with a friend right close to you all the time, skipping with you and keeping house with you and telling all her secrets to you, is about as far away as—as China is from an Enemy 'cross the fence! Oh, hum! some vacations are so splendid and some are so un-splendid!

It did not seem possible that anything drearier than this could happen. Margaret would not have dreamed it possible. But a little way farther down Lonesome Road waited something a great deal worse. It was waiting for Margaret behind the schoolhouse stone-wall. The very next day it jumped out upon her.

Usually at recess Nell—the Enemy—and Margaret had gone wandering away together with their arms around each other's waist, as happy as anything. But for a week of recesses now they had gone wandering in opposite directions—the Enemy marching due east, Margaret due west. The stone-wall stretched away to the west. She had found a nice lonesome little place to huddle in, behind the wall, out of sight. It was just the place to be miserable in.

"I know something!" from one of a little group of gossipers on the outside of the wall. "She needn't stick her chin out an' not come an' play with us. She's nothing but an adopted!"

"Oh!—a what?" in awestruck chorus from the listeners. "Say it again, Rhody Sharp."

"An adopted—that's all she is. I guess nobody but an adopted need to go trampin' past when we invite her to play with us! I guess we're good as she is an' better, too, so there!"

Margaret in her hidden nook heard with a cold terror creeping over her and settling around her heart. It was so close now that she breathed with difficulty. If—supposing they meant—

"Rhody Sharp, you're fibbing! I don't believe a single word you say!" sprang forth a champion valiantly. "She's dreadfully fond of her mother—just dreadfully!"

"She doesn't know it," promptly returned Rhody Sharp, her voice stabbing poor Margaret's ear like a sharp little sword. "They're keeping it from her. My gran'mother doesn't believe they'd ought to. She says—"

But nobody cared what Rhody Sharp's gran'mother said. A clatter of shocked little voices burst forth into excited, pitying discussion of the unfortunate who was nothing but an adopted. One of their own number! One they spelled with and multiplied with and said the capitals with every day! That they had invited to come and play with them—an' she'd stuck her chin out!

"Why! Why, then she's a—orphan!" one voice exclaimed. "Really an' honest she is—an' she doesn't know it!"

"Oh my, isn't it awful!" another voice. "Shouldn't you think she'd hide her head—I mean, if she knew?"

It was already hidden. Deep down in the sweet, moist grass—a little heavy, uncrowned, terror-smitten head. The cruel voices kept on.

"It's just like a disgrace, isn't it? Shouldn't you s'pose it would feel that way if 'twas you?"

"Think o' kissin' your mother good-night an' it's not bein' your mother?"

"Say, Rhody Sharp—all o' you—look here! Do you suppose that's why her mother—I mean she that isn't—dresses her in checked aperns? That's what orphans—"

The shorn head dug deeper. A soft groan escaped Margaret's lips. This very minute, now while she crouched in the grass,—oh, if she put out her hands and felt she would feel the checks! She had been to an orph—to a place once with Moth—with Her and seen the aprons herself. They were all—all checked.

At home, folded in a beautiful pile, there were all the others. There was the pink-checked one and the brown-checked one and the prettiest one of all, the one with teenty little white checks marked off with buff. The one she should feel if she put out her hand was a blue-checked.

Margaret drove her hands deep into the matted grass; she would not put them out. It was—it was terrible! Now she understood it all. She remembered—things. They crowded—with capital T's, Things,—up to her and pointed their fingers at her, and smiled dreadful smiles at her, and whispered to one another about her. They sat down on her and jounced up and down, till she gasped for breath.

The teacher's bell rang crisply and the voices changed to scampering feet. But Margaret crouched on in the sweet, moist grass behind the wall. She stayed there a week—a month—a year,—or was it only till the night chill stole into her bones and she crept away home?

She and Nell—she and the Enemy—had been so proud to have aprons just alike and cut by the same dainty pattern. But now if she knew—if the Enemy knew! How ashamed it would make her to have on one like—like an adopted's! How she'd wish hers was stripes! Perhaps—oh, perhaps she would think it was fortunate that she was an enemy now.

But the worst Things that crowded up and scoffed and gibed were not Things that had to do with enemies. The worst-of-all Things had to do with a little, tender woman with glasses on—whose hair didn't curl. Those Things broke Margaret's heart.

"Now you know why She makes you make the bed over again when it's wrinkly," gibed one Thing.

"And why she makes you mend the holes in your stockings," another Thing.

"She doesn't make me do the biggest ones!" flashed Margaret, hotly, but she could not stem the tide of Things. It swirled in.

"Perhaps now you see why She makes you hem towels and wipe dishes—"

"And won't let you eat two pieces of pie—"

"Or one piece o' fruit-cake—"

"Maybe you remember now the times she's said, 'This is no little daughter of mine'?"

Margaret turned sharply. "That was only because I was naughty," she pleaded, strickenly, but she knew in her soul it wasn't "only because." She knew it was because. The terror within her was growing more terrible every moment.

Then came shame. Like the evilest of the evil Things it had been lurking in the background waiting its turn,—it was its turn now. Margaret stood quite still, ashamed. She could not name the strange feeling, for she had never been ashamed before, but she sat there a piteous little figure in the grip of it. It was awful to be only nine and feel like that! To shrink from going home past Mrs. Streeter's and the minister's and the Enemy's!—oh, most of all past the Enemy's!—for fear they'd look out of the window and say, "There goes an adopted!" Perhaps they'd point their fingers.—Margaret closed her eyes dizzily and saw Mrs. Streeter's plump one and the minister's lean one and the Enemy's short brown one, all pointing. She could feel something burning her on her forehead,—it was "Adopted," branded there.

The Enemy was worst. Margaret crept under the fence just before she got to the Enemy's house and went a weary, roundabout way home. She could not bear to have this dearest Enemy see her in her disgrace.

Moth—She That had Been—would be wondering why Margaret was late. If she looked sober out of her eyes and said, "This can't be my little girl, can it?" then Margaret would know for certain. That would be the final proof.

The chimney was in sight now,—now the roof,—now the kitchen door, and She That Had Been was in it! She was shading her eyes and looking for the little girl that wasn't hers. A sob rose in the little girl's throat, but she tramped steadily on. It did not occur to her to snatch off her hat and wave it, as little girls that belonged did. She had done it herself.

The kitchen door was very near indeed now. It did not seem to be Margaret that was moving, but the kitchen door. It seemed to be coming to meet her and bringing with it a dear slender figure. She looked up and saw the soberness in its dear eyes.

"This can't be my little girl, can—" but Margaret heard no more. With a muffled wail she fled past the slender figure, up-stairs, that she did not see at all, to her own little room. On the bed she lay and felt her heart break under her awful little checked apron. For now she knew for certain.

Two darknesses shut down about her, and in the heart-break of one she forgot to be afraid of the other. She had always before been afraid of the night-dark and imagined creepy steps coming along the hall and into the door. The things she imagined now were dreadfuler than that. This new dark was so much darker!

They thought she was asleep and let her lie there on her little bed alone. By-and-by would be time enough to probe gently for the childish trouble. Perhaps she would leave it behind her in her sleep.

Out-of-doors suddenly a new sound rose shrill above the crickets and the frogs. It was the Enemy singing "Glory, glory, hallelujah." That was the last straw. Margaret writhed deeper into the pillows. She knew what the rest of it was—"Glory, glory, hallelujah, 'tisn't me! My soul goes marching on!" She was out there singing that a-purpose!

In her desperate need for some one to lay her trouble to, Margaret "laid it to" the Enemy. A sudden, bitter, unreasoning resentment took possession of her. If there hadn't been an Enemy, there wouldn't have been a trouble. Everything would have been beautiful and—and respectable, just as it was before. She would have been out there singing "Glory, glory hallelujah," too.

"She's to blame—I hate her!" came muffledly from the pillows. "Oh, I do!—I can't help it, I do! I'm always going to hate her forevermore! She needn't have—"

Needn't have what? What had the little scape-goat out there in the twilight done? But Margaret was beyond reasoning now. "Mine enemy hath done it," was enough for her. If she lived a thousand years—if she lived two thousand—she would never speak to the Enemy again,—never forgive her,—never put her into her prayer again among the God blesses.

A plan formulated itself after a while in the dark little room. It was born of the travail of the child's soul. Something must be done—there was something she would do. She began it at once, huddled up against the window to catch the failing light. She would pin it to her pincushion where they would find it after—after she was gone. Did folks ever mourn for an Adopted? In her sore heart Margaret yearned to have them mourn.

"I have found it out," she wrote with her trembling little fingers. "I don't suppose its wicked becaus I couldent help being one but it is orful. It breaks your hart to find youre one all of a suddin. If I had known before, I would have darned the big holes too. Ime going away becaus I canot bare living with folks I havent any right to. The stik pin this is pined on with is for Her That Wasent Ever my Mother for I love her still. When this you see remember me the rose is red the violet blue sugger is sweet and so are you.

"Margaret."

She pinned it on tremblingly and then crept back to bed. Perhaps she went to sleep,—at any rate, quite suddenly there were voices at her door—Her voice and—His. She did not stir, but lay and listened to them.

"Dear child! Wouldn't you wake her up, Henry? What do you suppose could have happened?" That was the voice that used to be Mother's. It made Margaret feel thrilly and homesick.

"Something at school, probably, dear,—you mustn't worry. All sorts of little troubles happen at school." The voice that used to be her Father's.

"I know, but this must have been a big one. If you had seen her little face, Henry! If she were Nelly, I should think somebody had been telling her—about her origin, you know—"

Margaret held her breath. Nelly was the Enemy, but what was an origin? This thing that they were saying—hark?

"I've always expected Nelly to find out that way—it would be so much kinder to tell her at home. You know it would, Henry, instead of letting her hear it from strangers and get her poor little heart broken. Henry, if God hadn't given us a precious little child of our own and we had ever adopted—"

Margaret dashed off the quilts and leaped to the floor with a cry of ecstasy. The anguish—the shame—the cruel gibing Things—were left behind her; they had slid from her burdened little heart at the first glorious rush of understanding; they would never come back,—never come back,—never come back to Margaret! Glory, glory, hallelujah, 'twasn't her! Her soul went marching on!

The two at the door suffered an unexpected, an amazing onslaught from a flying little figure. Its arms were out, were gathering them both in,—were strangling them in wild, exultant hugs.

"Oh! Oh, you're mine! I'm yours! We're each other's! I'm not an Adopted any more! I thought I was, and I wasn't! I was going away and die—oh, oh, oh!"

Then Margaret remembered the Enemy, and in the throes of her pity the enmity was swallowed up forever. The instant yearning that welled up in her to put her arms around the poor real Adopted almost stifled her. She slid out of the two pairs of big tender arms and scurried away like a hare. She was going to find Nelly and love her—oh, love her enough to make up! She would give her the coral beads she had always admired; she would let her be mistress and she'd be maid when they kept house,—she'd let her have the frosting half of all their cake and all the raisins.

"I'll let her wear the spangly veil when we dress up—oh, poor, poor Nelly!" Margaret cried softly as she ran. "And the longest trail. She may be the richest and have the most children—I'd rather."

There did not seem anything possible and beloved that she would not let Nelly do. She took agitated little leaps through the soft darkness, sending on ahead her yearning love in a tender little call: "Nelly! Nelly!"

She could never be too tender—too generous—to Nelly, to try to make up. And all her life she would take care of her and keep her from finding out. She shouldn't find out! When they were both, oh, very old, she would still be taking care of Nelly like that.

"Nelly! Nelly!"

If she could only think of some Great Thing she could do, that would—would hurt to do! And then she thought. She stopped quite suddenly in her impetuous rush, stilled by the Greatness of it.

"I'll let her love her mother the best," whispered Margaret to the stars,—"so there!"

Chapter IV

Bobby Unwelcome

Bobby had learned U that day in school, and he strutted home beside his nurse, Olga, with conscious relief in the swing of his sturdy legs. There was a special reason why Bobby felt relieved to get to U. He glanced up, up, up, sidewise, at the non-committal face so far above him, and wondered in his anxious little way whether or not it would be prudent to speak of the special reason now. Olga had times, Bobby had discovered, when you dassent speak of things, and it looked—yes, cert'nly—as though she was having one now. Still, if you only dast to—

"It's the same one that's in the middle o' my name, don't you know," he plunged in, hurriedly.

"Mercy! What iss it the child iss talking about!"

There! wasn't she having one? Didn't she usually say "Mercy!" like that when she was?

"That letter, you know—U. The one in the middle o' my name," Bobby hastened on—"right prezac'ly in the middle of it. I wish"—but he caught himself up with a jerk. It didn't seem best, after all, to consult Olga now—not now, while she was having one. Better wait—only, dear, dear, dear, how long he had waited a'ready!

It had not occurred to Bobby to consult his mother. They two were not intimately acquainted, and naturally he felt shy.

Bobby's mother was very young and beautiful. He had seen her dressed in a wondrous soft white dress once, with little specks of shiny things burning on her bare throat, and ever since he had known what angels look like.

There were reasons enough why Bobby seldom saw his mother. The house was very big, and her room so far away from his;—that was one reason. Then he always went to bed, and got up, and ate his meals before she did.

There was another reason why he and the beautiful young mother did not know each other very well, but even Olga had never explained that one. Bobby had that ahead of him to find out,—poor Bobby! Some one had called him Fire Face once at school, but the kind-hearted teacher had never let it happen again.

At home, in the great empty house, the mirrors were all high up out of reach, and in the nursery there had never been any at all. Bobby had never looked at himself in a mirror. Of course he had seen himself up to his chin—dear, yes—and admired his own little straight legs often enough, and doubled up his little round arms to hunt for his "muscle." In a quiet, unobtrusive way Bobby was rather proud of himself. He had to be—there was no one else, you see. And even at six, when there is so little else to do, one can put in considerable time regarding one's legs and arms.

"I guess you don't call those bow-legged legs, do you, Olga?" he had exulted once, in an unguarded moment when he had been thinking of Cleggy Munro's legs at school. "I guess you call those pretty straight-up-'n'-down ones!" And the hard face of the old nurse had suddenly softened in a strange, pleasant way, and for the one only time that he could remember, Olga had taken Bobby in her arms and kissed him.

"They're beautiful legs, that iss so," Olga had said, but she hadn't been looking at them when she said it. She had been looking straight into his face. The look hurt, too, Bobby remembered. He did not know what pity was, but it was that that hurt.

The night after he learned U at school Bobby decided to hazard everything and ask Olga what the one in his name stood for. He could not put it off any longer.

"Olga, what does the U in the middle o' my name stand for?" he broke out, suddenly, while he was being unbuttoned for bed. "I know it's a U, but I don't know a U-what. I've 'cided I won't go to bed till I've found out."

Things had gone criss-cross. The old Norwegian woman was not in a good humor.

"Unwelcome—that iss what it must stand for," she laughed unpleasantly.

"Bobby Unwelcome!" Bobby laughed too. Then a piteous little suspicion crept into his mind and began to grow. He turned upon Olga sharply. "What does Unwelcome mean?" he demanded.

"Eh? Iss it not enough plain to you? Well, not wanted—that iss what it means then."

"Not wanted,—not wanted." Bobby repeated the words over and over to himself, not quite satisfied yet. They sounded bad—oh, very; but perhaps Olga had got them wrong. She was not a United States person. It would be easy for another kind of a person to get things wrong. Still—"not wanted"—they certainly sounded very plain. And they meant—Bobby gave a faint gasp, and suddenly his thoughts turned dizzily round and round one terrible pivot—"not wanted." He sprang away out of the nurse's hands and darted down the long, bright hall to his mother's room. She was being dressed for a ball, and the room was pitilessly light. She sat at a table with a little mirror before her. Suddenly another face appeared in it with hers—a little, scarred, red face, stamped deep with childish woe. The contrast appalled her.

Bobby was not looking into the glass, but into her beautiful face.

"Is that what it stands for?" he demanded, breathlessly. "She said so. Did she lie?"

"Robert! For Heaven's sake, child, stand away! You are tearing my lace. What are you doing here? Why are you not in bed?"

"Does it stand for that?" he persisted.

"Does what stand for what? Look, you are crushing my dress. Stand farther off. Don't you see, child?"

"She said the U in the middle o' my name stood for Not Wanted. Does it? Tell me quick. Does it?"

The contrast of the two faces in her mirror hurt her like a blow. It brought back all the disappointment and the wounded vanity of that time, six years ago, when they had shown her the tiny, disfigured face of her son.

"No, it wasn't that. I morember now. It was Unwelcome, but it means that. Is the middle o' my name Unwelcome—what?"

"Oh yes, yes, yes!" she cried, scarcely knowing what she said. The boy's eyes followed hers to the mirror, and in that brief, awful space he tasted of the Tree of Knowledge.

With a little cry he stumbled backward into the lighted hall. There was a slip, and the sound of a soft little body bounding down the polished stairs.

A good while afterwards Bobby opened his eyes wonderingly. There seemed to be people near him, but he could not see them at all distinctly. A faint, wonderful perfume crept to him.

"It's very dark, isn't it?" he said, in surprise. "I can smell a beautiful smell, but I can't see it. Why, why! It isn't you, is it?—not my mother? Why, I wasn't 'specting to find— Oh, I morember it now—I morember it all! Then I'm glad it's dark. I shouldn't want it to be as light as that again. Oh no! oh no! I shouldn't want her to see— Why, she's crying! What is she crying for?"

He put out a small weak hand and groped towards the sound of bitter sobbing. Instinctively he knew it was she.

"I'm very sorry. I guess I know what the matter is. It's me, and I'm very sorry. I never knew it before; no, I never. I'm glad it's dark now—aren't you?—'count o' that. Only I'm a little speck sorry it isn't light enough for you to see my legs. They're very straight ones—you can ask Olga. You might feel of 'em if you thought 'twould help any to. P'r'aps it might make you feel a very little—just a very little—better to. They're cert'nly very straight ones. But then of course they aren't like a—like a—a face. They're only legs. But they're the best I can do."

He ended wearily, with a sigh of pain. The bitter sobbing kept on, and seemed to trouble him. Then a new idea occurred to him, and he made a painful effort to turn on his pillow and to speak brightly.

"I didn't think of that— P'r'aps you think I'm feeling bad 'count o' the U in the middle o' my name. Is that what makes you cry? Why, you needn't. That's all right! After—after I looked in there, of course I knew 'bout how it was. I wish you wouldn't cry. It joggles my—my heart."

But it was his little broken body that it joggled. The mother found it out, and stopped sobbing by a mighty effort. She drew very close to Bobby in the dark that was light to every one else, and laid her wet cheek against the little, scarred, red face. The motion was so gentle that it scarcely stirred the yellow tendrils of his soft hair. An infinite tenderness was born out of her anguish. There was left her a merciful moment to be a mother in. Bobby forgot his pain in the bliss of it.

"Why, why, this is very nice!" he murmured, happily. "I never knew it would be as nice as this—I never knew! But I'm glad it's dark,—aren't you? I'd rather it would—be——dark."

And then it grew altogether dark for Bobby, and the little face against the new-born, heart-broken mother's cheek felt cold, and would not warm with all her passionate kisses.

Chapter V

The Little Girl Who Should Have Been a Boy

There was so much time for the Little Girl who should have been a Boy to ponder over it. She was only seven, but she grew quite skilful in pondering. After lessons—and lessons were over at eleven—there was the whole of the rest of the day to wander, in her little, desolate way, in the gardens. She liked the fruit-garden best, and the Golden Pippin tree was her choicest pondering-place. There was never any one there with her. The Little Girl who should have been a Boy was always alone.

"You see how it is. I've told you times enough," she communed with herself, in her quaint, unchildish fashion. "You are a mistake. You went and was born a Girl, when they wanted a Boy—oh, my, how they wanted a Boy! But the moment they saw you they knew it was all up with them. You wasn't wicked, really,—I guess it wasn't wicked; sometimes I can't be certain,—but you did go and make such a silly mistake! Look at me,—why didn't you know how much they wanted a Boy and didn't want you? Why didn't you be brave and go up to the Head Angel, and say, 'Send me to another place; for pity sake don't send me there. They want a Little Boy.' Why didn't you—oh, why didn't you? It would have saved such a lot of trouble!"

The Little Girl who should have been a Boy always sighed at that point. The sigh made a period to the sad little speech, for after that she always sat in the long grass under the Golden Pippin tree and rocked herself back and forth silently. There was no use in saying anything more after that. It had all been said.

It was a great, beautiful estate, to east and west and north and south of her, and the Boy the Head Angel should have sent instead of the sad Little Girl was to have inherited it all. And there was a splendid title that went with the estate. In the sharp mind of the Little Girl nothing was hidden or undiscovered.

"It seems a pity to have it wasted," she mused, wistfully, with her grave wide eyes on the beautiful green expanses all about her, "just for a mistake like that,—I mean like me—too. You'd think the Head Angel would be ashamed of himself, wouldn't you? He prob'ly is."

The Shining Mother—it was thus the Little Girl who should have been a Boy had named her, on account of her sparkling eyes and wonderful sparkling gowns; everything about the Shining Mother sparkled—the Shining Mother was almost always away. So was the Ogre. Somewhere outside—clear outside—of the green expanses there was a gay, frivolous world where almost always they two stayed.

The Little Girl called her father the Ogre for want of a better name. She was never quite satisfied with the name, but it had to answer till she found another. Prob'ly ogres didn't wear an eye-glass in one of their eyes, or flip off the sweet little daisy heads with cruel canes, but they were oldish and scare-ish, and of course they wouldn't have noticed you any, even if you were their Little Girl. Ogres would have prob'ly wanted a Boy too, and that's the way they'd have let you see your mistake. So, till she found a better name, the Little Girl who had made the mistake called her father the Ogre. She was very proud and fond of the Shining Mother, but she was a little afraid of the Ogre. After all, one feeling mattered about as much as the other.

"It doesn't hurt you any to be afraid, when you do it all alone by yourself," she reasoned, "and it doesn't do you any good to be fond. It only amuses you," she added, with sad wisdom. As I said, she was only seven, but she was very old indeed.

So the time went along until the weeks piled up into months. The summer she was eight, the Little Girl could not stand it any longer. She decided that something must be done. The Shining Mother and the Ogre were coming back to the green expanses. She had found that out at lessons.

"And then they will have it all to go over again—all the miser'bleness of my not being a Boy," the Little Girl thought, sadly. "And I don't know whether they can stand it or not, but I can't."

A wave of infinite longing had swept over the shy, sensitive soul of the Little Girl who should have been a Boy. One of two things must happen—she must be loved, or die. So, being desperate, she resolved to chance everything. It was under the Golden Pippin tree, rocking herself back and forth in the long grass, that she made her plans. Straight on the heels of them she went to the gardener's little boy.

"Lend me—no, I mean give me—your best clothes," she said, with gentle imperiousness. It was not a time to waste words. At best, the time that was left to practise in was limited enough.

"Your best clothes," she had said, realizing distinctly that fustian and corduroy would not do. She was even a little doubtful of the best clothes. The gardener's little boy, once his mouth had shut and his legs come back to their locomotion, brought them at once. If there was a suspicion of alacrity in his obedience towards the last, it escaped the thoughtful eyes of the Little Girl. Having always been a mistake, nothing more, how could she know that a boy's best clothes are not always his dearest possession? Now if it had been the threadbare, roomy, easy little fustians, with their precious pocket-loads, that she had demanded!

There were six days left to practise in—only six. How the Little Girl practised! It was always quite alone by herself. She did it in a sensible, orderly way,—the leaps and strides first, whoops next, whistle last. The gardener's little boy's best clothes she kept hidden in the long grass, under the Golden Pippin tree, and on the fourth day she put them on. Oh, the agony of the fourth day! She came out of that practice period a wan, white, worn little thing that should never have been a Boy.

For it was heart-breaking work. Every instinct of the Little Girl's rebelled against it. It was terrible to leap and whoop and whistle; her very soul revolted. But it was life or death to her, and always she persevered.

In those days lessons scarcely paid. They were only a pitiful makeshift. The Little Girl lived only in her terrible practice hours. She could not eat or sleep. She grew thin and weak.

"I don't look like me at all," she told herself, on a chair before her mirror. "But that isn't the worst of it. I don't look like the Boy, either. Ugh! how I look! I wonder if the Angel would know me? It would be kind of dreadful not to have anybody know you. Well, you won't be you when you're the Boy, so prob'ly it won't matter."

On the sixth day—the last thing—she cut her hair off. She did it with her eyes shut to give herself courage, but the snips of the shears broke her heart. The Little Girl had always loved her soft, shining hair. It had been like a beautiful thing apart from her, that she could caress and pet. She had made an idol of it, having nothing else to love.

When it was all shorn off she crept out of the room without opening her eyes. After that the gardener's little boy's best clothes came easier to her, she found. And she could whoop and leap and whistle a little better. It was almost as if she had really made herself the Boy she should have been.

Then the Shining Mother came, and the Ogre. The Little Girl—I mean the Boy—was waiting for them, swinging her—his—feet from a high branch of the Golden Pippin tree. He was whistling.

"But I think I am going to die," he thought, behind the whistle. "I'm certain I am. I feel it coming on."

Of course, after a little, there was a hunt everywhere for the Little Girl. Even little girls cannot slip out of existence like that, undiscovered. The beautiful green expanses were hunted over and over, but only a gardener's little boy in his best clothes, whistling faintly, was found. He fell out of the Golden Pippin tree as the field-servants went by, and they stopped to carry his limp little figure to the gardener's lodge. Then the hunt went forward again. The Shining Mother grew faint and sick with fear, and the Ogre strode about like one demented. It was hardly what was to be expected of the Shining Mother and the Ogre.

Towards night the mystery was partly solved. It was the Shining Mother who found the connecting threads. She found the little, jagged locks of soft, sweet hair. The Ogre came upon her sitting on the floor among them, and the whiteness of her face terrified him.

"I know—you need not tell me what has happened!" she said, scarcely above a whisper, as if in the presence of the dead. "A door in me has opened, and I see it all—all, I tell you! We have never had her,—and now, dear God in heaven, we have lost her!"

It was very nearly so. They could hardly know then how near it came to being true. Link by link they came upon the little chain of pitiful proofs. They found all the little, sweet, white girl-clothes folded neatly by themselves and laid in a pile together, as if on an altar for sacrifice. If the Little Girl had written "Good-bye" in her childish scrawl upon them, the Shining Mother would not have better understood. So many things she was seeing beyond that open door.

They found the Little Girl's dolls laid out like little, white-draped corpses in one of her bureau-drawers. The row of stolid little faces gazed up at them with the mystery of the Sphinx in all their glittering eyes. It was the Shining Mother who shut the drawer, but first she kissed the faces.

After all, the Ogre discovered the last little link of the chain. He brought it home in his arms from the gardener's lodge, and laid it on the Little Girl's white bed. It was very still and pitiful and small. The took the gardener's little boy's best clothes off from it and put on the soft white night-gown of the Little Girl. Then, one on one side and one on the other, they kept their long hard vigil.

It was night when the Little Girl opened her eyes, and the first thing they saw was the chairful of little girl-clothes the Shining Mother had set beside the bed. Then they saw the Shining Mother. Things came back to the Little Girl by slow degrees. But the look in the Shining Mother's face—that did not come back. That had never been there before. The Little Girl, in her wise, old way, understood that look, and gasped weakly with the joy and wonder of it. Oh, the joy! Oh, the wonder!

"But I tried to be one," she whispered after a while, a little bewildered still. "I should have done it, if I hadn't died. I couldn't help that; I felt it coming on. Prob'ly, though, I shouldn't have made a very good one."

The Shining Mother bent over and took the Little Girl in her arms.

"Dear," she whispered, "it was the Boy that died. I am glad he died."

So, though the Ogre and the Shining Mother had not found their Boy, the Little Girl had found a father and mother.

Chapter VI

The Lie

The Lie went up to bed with him. Russy didn't want it to, but it crept in through the key-hole,—it must have been the key-hole, for the door was shut the minute Metta's skirt had whisked through. But one thing Russy had to be thankful for,—Metta didn't know it was there in the room. As far as that went, it was a kind-hearted Lie. But after Metta went away,—after she had put out the light and said "Pleasant dreams, Master Russy, an' be sure an' don't roll out,"—after that!

Russy snuggled deep down in the pillows and said he would go right to sleep; oh, right straight! He always had before. It made you forget the light was out, and there were queer, creaky night-noises all round your bed,—under it some of 'em; over by the bureau some of 'em; and some of 'em coming creepy, cree-py up the stairs. You dug your head deep down in the pillows, and the next thing you knew you were asleep,—no, awake, and the noises were beautiful day-ones that you liked. You heard roosters crowing, and Mr. Vandervoort's cows calling for breakfast, and, likely as not, some mother-birds singing duets with their husbands. Oh yes, it was a good deal the best way to do, to go right straight to sleep when Metta put the light out.

But to-night it was different, for the Lie was there. You couldn't go to sleep with a Lie in the room. It was worse than creepy, creaky noises,—mercy, yes! You'd swap it for those quick enough and not ask a single bit of "boot." You almost wanted to hear the noises.

It came across the room. There was no sound, but Russy knew it was coming well enough. He knew when it got up close to the side of the bed. Then it stopped and began to speak. It wasn't "out loud" and it wasn't a whisper, but Russy heard it.

"Move over; I'm coming into bed with you," the Lie said. "I hope you don't think I'm going to sit up all night. Besides, I'm always scared in the dark,—it runs in my family. The Lies are always afraid. They're not good sleepers, either, so let's talk. You begin—or shall I?"

"You," moaned Russy.

"Well, I say, this is great, isn't it! I like this house. I stayed at Barney Toole's last night and it doesn't begin with this. Barney's folks are poor, and there aren't any curtains or carpets or anything,—nor pillows on the bed. I never slept a wink at Barney's. I'm hoping I shall drop off here, after a while. It's a new place, and I'm more likely to in new places. You never slept with one o' my family before, did you?"

"No," Russy groaned. "Oh no, I never before!"

"That's what I thought. I should have been likely to hear of it if you had. I was a little surprised,—I say, what made you have anything to do with me. I was never more surprised in my life! They'd always said: 'Well, you'll never get acquainted with that Russy Rand. He's another kind.' Then you went and shook hands with me!"

"I had to." Russy sat up in bed and stiffened himself for self-defence. "I had to! When Jeffy Vandervoort said that about Her,—well, I guess you'd have had to if they said things about your mother—"

"I never had one. The Lies have a Father, that's all. Go ahead."

"There isn't anything else,—I just had to."

"Tell what you said and what he said. Go ahead."

"You know all about—"

"Go ahead!"

Russy rocked himself back and forth in his agony. It was dreadful to have to say it all over again.

"Well, then," doggedly, "Jeffy said my mother never did, but his did—oh, always!"

"Did what—oh, always?"

Russy clinched his little round fingers till the bones cracked under the soft flesh.

"Kissed him good-night—went up to his room a-purpose to, an'—an'—tucked him in. Oh, always, he said. He said mine never did. An' I said—"

"You said—go ahead!"

"I said she did, too,—oh—always," breathed Russy in the awful dark. "I had to. When it's your mother, you have to—"

"I never had one, I told you! How do I know? Go on."

He was driven on relentlessly. He had it all to go through with, and he whispered the rest hurriedly to get it done.

"I said she tucked me in,—came up a-purpose to,—an' always kissed me twice (his only does once), an' always—called me—Dear." Russy fell back in a heap on the pillows and sobbed into them.

"My badness!"—anybody but a Lie would have said "my goodness,"—"but you did do it up brown that time, didn't you! But I don't suppose he believed a word of it—you didn't make him believe you, did you?"

"He had to," cried out Russy, fiercely. "He said I'd never lied to him in my life—"

"Before;—yes, I know."

Russy slipped out of bed and padded over the thick carpet towards the place where the window-seat was in the daytime. But it wasn't there. He put out his hands and hunted desperately for it. Yes, there,—no, that was sharp and hard and hurt you. That must be the edge of the bureau. He tried again, for he must find it,—he must! He would not stay in bed with that Lie another minute. It crowded him,—it tortured him so.

"This is it," thought Russy, and sank down gratefully on the cushions. His bare feet scarcely touched toe-tips to the floor. Here he would stay all night. This was better than—

"I'm coming,—which way are you? Can't you speak up?"

The Lie was coming, too! Suddenly an awful thought flashed across Russy's little, weary brain. What if the Lie would always come, too? What if he could never get away from it? What if it slept with him, walked with him, talked with him, lived with him,—oh, always!

But Russy stiffened again with dogged courage. "I had to!" he thought. "I had to,—I had to,—I had to! When he said things about Her,—when it's your mother,—you have to."

A great time went by, measureless by clock-ticks and aching little heart-beats. It seemed to be weeks and months to Russy. Then he began to feel a slow relief creeping over his misery, and he said to himself the Lie must have "dropped off." There was not a sound of it in the room. It grew so still and beautiful that Russy laughed to himself in his relief. He wanted to leap to his feet and dance about the room, but he thought of the sharp corners and hard edges of things in time. Instead, he nestled among the cushions of the window-seat and laughed on softly. Perhaps it was all over,—perhaps it wasn't asleep, but had gone away—to Barney Toole's, perhaps, where they regularly "put up" Lies,—and would never come back! Russy gasped for joy. Perhaps when you'd never shaken hands with a Lie but once in your life, and that time you had to, and you'd borne it, anyway, for what seemed like weeks and months,—perhaps then they went away and left you in peace! Perhaps you'd had punishment enough then.

Very late Russy's mother came up-stairs. She was very tired, and her pretty young face in the frame of soft down about her opera-cloak looked a little cross. Russy's father plodded behind more heavily.

"The boy's room, Ellen?—just this once?" he pleaded in her ear. "It will take but a minute."

"I am so tired, Carter! Well, if I must— Why, he isn't in the bed!"

The light from the hall streamed in, showing it tumbled and tossed as if two had slept in it. But no one was in it now. The mother's little cry of surprise sharpened to anxiety.

"Where is he, Carter? Why don't you speak? He isn't here in bed, I tell you! Russy isn't here!"

"He has rolled out,—no, he hasn't rolled out. I'll light up—there he is, Ellen! There's the little chap on the window-seat!"

"And the window is open!" she cried, sharply. She darted across to the little figure and gathered it up into her arms. She had never been frightened about Russy before. Perhaps it was the fright that brought her to her own.

"He is cold,—his little night-dress is damp!" she said. Then her kisses rained down on the little, sleeping face. In his sleep, Russy felt them, but he thought it was Jeffy's mother kissing Jeffy.

"It feels good, doesn't it?" he murmured. "I don't wonder Jeffy likes it! If my mother kissed me— I told Jeffy she did! It was a Lie, but I had to. You have to, when they say things like that about your mother. You have to say she kisses you—oh, always! She comes 'way up-stairs every night a-purpose to. An' she tucks you in, an' she calls you—Dear. It's a Lie an' it 'most kills you, but you have to say it. But it's perfectly awful afterwards." He nestled against the soft down of her cloak and moaned as if in pain. "It's awful afterwards when you have to sleep with the Lie. It's perfectly—aw—ful—"

"Oh, Carter!" the mother broke out, for it was all plain to her. In a flash of agonized understanding the wistful little sleep-story was filled out in every detail. She understood all the tragedy of it.

"Russy! Russy!" She shook him in her eagerness. "Russy, it's my kisses! I'm kissing you! It isn't Jeffy's mother,—it's your mother, Russy! Feel them!—don't you feel them on your forehead and your hair and your little red lips? It's your mother kissing you!"

Russy opened his eyes.

"Why! Why, so it is!" he said.

"And calling you 'Dear,' Russy! Don't you hear her? Dear boy,—dear little boy! You hear her, don't you, Russy—dear?"

"Why, yes!—why!"

"And tucking you into bed—like this,—so! She's tucking in the blanket now,—and now the little quilt, Russy! That is what mothers are for—I never thought before—oh, I never thought!" She dropped her face beside his on the pillow and fell to kissing him again. He held his face quite still for the sweet, strange baptism. Then suddenly he laughed out happily, wildly.

"Then it isn't a Lie!" he cried, in a delirium of relief and joy. "It's true!"

Chapter VII

The Princess of Make-Believe

The Princess was washing dishes. On her feet she would barely have reached the rim of the great dish-pan, but on the soap-box she did very well. A grimy calico apron trailed to the floor.

"Now this golden platter I must wash extry clean," the Princess said. "The Queen is ve-ry particular about her golden platters. Last time, when I left one o' the corners—it's such a nextremely heavy platter to hold—she gave me a scold—oh, I mean—I mean she tapped me a little love pat on my cheek with her golden spoon."

It was a great, brown-veined, stoneware platter, and the arms of the Princess ached with holding it. Then, in an unwary instant, it slipped out of her soapsudsy little fingers and crashed to the floor. Oh! oh! the Queen! the Queen! She was coming! The Princess heard her shrill, angry voice, and felt the jar of her heavy steps. There was the space of an instant—an instant is so short!—before the storm broke.

"You little limb o' Satan! That's my best platter, is it? Broke all to bits, eh? I'll break—" But there was a flurry of dingy apron and dingier petticoats, and the little Princess had fled. She did not stop till she was in her Secret Place among the willows. Her small lean face was pale but undaunted.

"Th-the Queen isn't feeling very well to-day," she panted. "It's wash-day up at the Castle. She never enjoys herself on wash-days. And then that golden platter—I'm sorry I smashed it all to flinders! When the Prince comes I shall ask him to buy another."

The Prince had never come, but the Princess waited for him patiently. She sat with her face to the west and looked for him to come through the willows with the red sunset light filtering across his hair. That was the way the Prince was coming, though the time was not set. It might be a good while before he came, and then again—you never could tell!

"But when he does, and we've had a little while to get acquainted, then I shall say to him, 'Hear, O Prince, and give ear to my—my petition! For verily, verily, I have broken many golden platters and jasper cups and saucers, and the Queen, long live her! is sore—sore—'"

The Princess pondered for the forgotten word. She put up a little lean brown hand and rubbed a tingling spot on her temple—ah, not the Queen! It was the Princess—long live her!—who was "sore."

"'I beseech thee, O Prince,' I shall say, 'buy new golden platters and jasper cups and saucers for the Queen, and then shall I verily, verily be—be—'"

Oh, the long words—how they slipped out of reach! The little Princess sighed rather wearily. She would have to rehearse that speech so many times before the Prince came. Suppose he came to-night! Suppose she looked up now, this minute, towards the golden west and he was there, swinging along through the willow canes towards her!

But there was no one swinging along through the willows. The yellow light flickered through—that was all. Somewhere, a long way off, sounded the monotonous hum of men's voices. Through the lace-work of willow twigs there showed the faintest possible blur of color. Down beyond, in the clearing, the Castle Guards in blue jean blouses were pulling stumps. The Princess could not see their dull, passionless faces, and she was glad of it. The Castle Guards depressed her. But they were not as bad as the Castle Guardesses. They were mostly old women with bleared, dim eyes, and they wore such faded—silks.

"My silk dress is rather faded," murmured the little Princess wistfully. She smoothed down the scant calico skirt with her brown little fingers. The patch in it she would not see.

"I shall have to have the Royal Dress-maker make me another one soon. Let me see,—what color shall I choose? I'd like my gold-colored velvet made up. I'm tired of wearing royal purple dresses all the time, though of course I know they're appropriater. I wonder what color the Prince would like best? I should rather choose that color."

The Princess's little brown hands were clasped about one knee, and she was rocking herself slowly back and forth, her eyes, wistful and wide, on the path the Prince would come. She was tired to-day and it was harder to wait.

"But when he comes I shall say, 'Hear, O Prince. Verily, verily, I did not know which color you would like to find me dressed—I mean arrayed—in, and so I beseech thee excuse—pardon, I mean—mine infirmity.'"

The Princess was not sure of "infirmity," but it sounded well. She could not think of a better word.

"And then—I think then—he will take me in his arms, and his face will be all sweet and splendid like the Mother o' God's in the picture, and he will whisper,—I don't think he will say it out loud,—oh, I'd rather not!—'Verily, Princess,' he will whisper, 'Oh, verily, verily, thou hast found favor in my sight!' And that will mean that he doesn't care what color I am, for he—loves—me."

Lower and lower sank the solemn voice of the Princess. Slower and slower rocked the little, lean body. The birds themselves stopped singing at the end. In the Secret Place it was very still.

"Oh no, no, no,—not verily!" breathed the Princess, in soft awe. For the wonder of it took her breath away. She had never in her life been loved, and now, at this moment, it seemed so near! She thought she heard the footsteps of the Prince.

They came nearer. The crisp twigs snapped under his feet. He was whistling.

"Oh, I can't look!—I can't!" gasped the little Princess, but she turned her face to the west,—she had always known it would be from the west, and lifted closed eyes to his coming. When he got to the Twisted Willow she might dare to look,—to the Little Willow Twins, anyway.

"And I shall know when he does," she thought. "I shall know the minute!"

Her face was rapt and tender. The miracle she had made for herself,—the gold she had coined out of her piteous alloy,—was it not come true at last?—Verily, verily?

Hush! Was the Prince not coming through the willows? And the sunshine was trickling down on his hair! The Princess knew, though she did not look.

"He is at the Twisted Willow," she thought. "Now he is at the Little Willow Twins." But she did not open her eyes. She did not dare. This was a little different, she had never counted on being afraid.

The twigs snapped louder and nearer—now very near. The merry whistle grew clearer, and then it stopped.

"Hullo!"

Did princes say "hullo!" The Princess had little time to wonder, for he was there before her. She could feel his presence in every fibre of her trembling little being, though she would not open her eyes for very fear that it might be somebody else. No, no, it was the Prince! It was his voice, clear and ringing, as she had known it would be. She put up her hands suddenly and covered her eyes with them to make surer. It was not fear now, but a device to put off a little longer the delight of seeing him.

"I say, hullo! Haven't you got any tongue?"

"Oh, verily, verily,—I mean hear, O Prince, I beseech," she panted. The boy's merry eyes regarded the shabby small person in puzzled astonishment. He felt an impulse to laugh and run away, but his royal blood forbade either. So he waited.

"You are the Prince," the little Princess cried. "I've been waiting the longest time,—but I knew you'd come," she added, simply. "Have you got your velvet an' gold buckles on? I'm goin' to look in a minute, but I'm waiting to make it spend."

The Prince whistled softly. "No," he said then, "I didn't wear them clo'es to-day. You see, my mother—"

"The Queen," she interrupted, "you mean the Queen?"

"You bet I do! She's a reg'lar-builter! Well, she don't like to have me wearin' out my best clo'es every day," he said, gravely.

"No," eagerly, "nor mine don't. Queen, I mean,—but she isn't a mother, mercy, no! I only wear silk dresses every day, not my velvet ones. This silk one is getting a little faded." She released one hand to smooth the dress wistfully. Then she remembered her painfully practised little speech and launched into it hurriedly.

"Hear, O Prince. Verily, verily, I did not know which color you'd like to find me dressed in—I mean arrayed. I beseech thee to excuse—oh, pardon, I mean—"

But she got no further. She could endure the delay no longer, and her eyes flew open.

She had known his step; she had known his voice. She knew his face. It was terribly freckled, and she had not expected freckles on the face of the Prince. But the merry, honest eyes were the Prince's eyes. Her gaze wandered downward to the home-made clothes and bare, brown legs, but without uneasiness. The Prince had explained about his clothes. Suddenly, with a shy, glad little cry, the Princess held out her hands to him.

The royal blood flooded the face of the Prince and filled in all the spaces between its little, gold-brown freckles. But the Prince held out his hand to her. His lips formed for words and she thought he was going to say, "Verily, Princess, thou hast found favor—"

"Le' 's go fishin'," the Prince said.

Chapter VIII

The Promise

Murray was not as one without hope, for there was the Promise. The remembrance of it set him now to exulting, in an odd, restrained little way, where a moment ago he had been desponding. He clasped plump, brown little hands around a plump, brown little knee and swayed gently this way and that.

"Maybe she'll begin with my shoes," Murray thought, and held his foot quite still. He could almost feel light fingers unlacing the stubbed little shoe; Sheelah's fingers were rather heavy and not patient with knots. Hers would be patient—there are some things one is certain of.

"When she unbuttons me," Murray mused on, sitting absolutely motionless, as if she were unbuttoning him now—"when she unbuttons me I shall hold in my breath—this way," though he could hardly have explained why.

She had never unlaced or unbuttoned him. Always, since he was a little, breathing soul, it had been Sheelah. It had never occurred to him that he loved Sheelah, but he was used to her. All the mothering he had ever experienced had been the Sheelah kind—thorough enough, but lacking something; Murray was conscious that it lacked something. Perhaps—perhaps to-night he should find out what. For to-night not Sheelah, but his mother, was going to undress him and put him to bed. She had promised.

It had come about through his unprecedented wail of grief at parting, when she had gone into the nursery to say good-bye, in her light, sweet way. Perhaps it was because she was to be gone all day; perhaps he was a little lonelier than usual. He was always rather a lonely little boy, but there were worse times; perhaps this had been a worse time. Whatever had been the reason that prompted him, he had with disquieting suddenness, before Sheelah could prevent it, flung his arms about the pretty mother and made audible objection to her going.

"Why, Murray!" She had been taken by surprise. "Why, you little silly! I'm coming back to-night; I'm only going for the day! You wouldn't see much more of me if I stayed at home." Which, from its very reasonableness, had quieted him. Of course he would not see much more of her. As suddenly as he had wailed he stopped wailing. Yet she had promised. Something had sent her back to the nursery door to do it.

"Be a good boy and I'll come home before you go to bed! I'll put you to bed," she had promised. "We'll have a regular lark!"

Hence he was out here on the door-step being a good boy. That Sheelah had taken unfair advantage of the Promise and made the being good rather a perilous undertaking, he did not appreciate. He only knew he must walk a narrow path across a long, lonely day.

There were certain things—one especial certain thing—he wanted to know, but instinct warned him not to interrupt Sheelah till her work was done, or she might call it not being good. So he waited, and while he waited he found out the special thing. An unexpected providence sent enlightenment his way, to sit down beside him on the door-step. Its other name was Daisy.

"Hullo, Murray! Is it you?" Daisy, being of the right sex, asked needless questions sometimes.

"Yes," answered Murray, politely.

"Well, le's play. I can stay half a hour. Le's tag."

"I can't play," rejoined Murray, caution restraining his natural desires. "I'm being good."

"Oh, my!" shrilled the girl child derisively. "Can't you be good tagging? Come on."

"No; because you might—I might get no-fairing, and then Sheelah'd come out and say I was bad. Le's sit here and talk; it's safer to. What's a lark, Daisy? I was going to ask Sheelah."

"A—lark? Why, it's a bird, of course!"

"I don't mean the bird kind, but the kind you have when your mother puts you—when something splendid happens. That kind, I mean."

Daisy pondered. Her acquaintance with larks was limited, unless it meant—

"Do you mean a good time?" she asked. "We have larks over to my house when we go to bed—"

"That's it! That's the kind!" shouted delighted Murray. "I'm going to have one when I go to bed. Do you have reg'lar ones, Daisy?" with a secret little hope that she didn't. "I'm going to have a reg'lar one."

"Huh!—chase all 'round the room an' turn somersaults an' be highway robberers? An' take the hair-pins out o' your mother's hair an' hide in it—what?"

Murray gasped a little at the picture of that kind of a lark. It was difficult to imagine himself chasing 'round the room or being a highwayman; and as for somersaults—he glanced uneasily over his shoulder, as if Sheelah might be looking and read "somersaults" through the back of his head. For once he had almost turned one and Sheelah had found him in the middle of it and said pointed things. In Sheelah's code of etiquette there were no somersaults in the "s" column.

"It's a reg'lar lark to hide in your mother's hair," was going on the girl child's voice. "Yes, sir, that's the reg'larest kind!"

Murray gasped again, harder. For that kind took away his breath altogether and made him feel a little dizzy, as if he were—were doing it now—hiding in his mother's hair! It was soft, beautiful, gold-colored hair, and there was a great deal of it—oh, plenty to hide in! He shut his eyes and felt it all about him and soft against his face, and smelled the faint fragrance of it. The dizziness was sweet.

Yes, that must be the reg'larest kind of a lark, but Murray did not deceive himself, once the dream was over. He knew that kind was not waiting for him at the end of this long day. But a lark was waiting, anyway—a plain lark. It might have been the bird kind in his little heart now, singing for joy at the prospect.

Impatience seized upon Murray. He wanted this little neighbor's half-hour to be up, so that he could go in and watch the clock. He wanted Sheelah to come out here, for that would mean it was ten o'clock; she always came at ten. He wanted it to be noon, to be afternoon, to be night! The most beautiful time in his rather monotonous little life was down there at the foot of the day, and he was creeping towards it on the lagging hours. He was like a little traveller on a dreary plain, with the first ecstatic glimpse of a hill ahead.

Murray in his childish way had been in love a long time, but he had never got very near his dear lady. He had watched her a little way off and wondered at the gracious beauty of her, and loved her eyes and her lips and her soft, gold-colored hair. He had never—oh, never—been near enough to be unlaced and unbuttoned and put to bed by the lady that he loved. She had come in sometimes in a wondrous dress to say good night, but often, stopping at the mirror on the way across to him, she had seen a beautiful vision and forgotten to say it. And Murray had not wondered, for he had seen the vision, too.

"Your mamma's gone away, hasn't she? I saw her."

Daisy was still there! Murray pulled himself out of his dreaming, to be polite.

"Yes; but she's coming back to-night. She promised."

"S'posing the cars run off the track so she can't?" Daisy said, cheerfully.

"She'll come," Murray rejoined, with the decision of faith. "She promised, I said."

"S'posing she's killed 'most dead?"

"She'll come."

"Puffickly dead—s'posing?"

Murray took time, but even here his faith in the Promise stood its ground, though the ground shook under it. Sheelah had taught him what a promise was; it was something not to be shaken or killed even in a railroad wreck.

"When anybody promises, they do it," he said, sturdily. "She promised an' she'll come."

"Then her angel will have to come," remarked the older, girl child, coolly, with awful use of the indicative mood.

When the half-hour was over and Murray at liberty, he went in to the clock and stood before it with hands a-pocket and wide-spread legs. A great yearning was upon him to know the mystery of telling time. He wished—oh, how he wished he had let Sheelah teach him! Then he could have stood here making little addition sums and finding out just how long it would be till night. Or he could go away and keep coming back here to make little subtraction sums, to find out how much time was left now—and now—and now. It was dreadful to just stand and wonder things.

Once he went up-stairs to his own little room out of the nursery and sat down where he had always sat when Sheelah unlaced him, before he had begun to unlace himself, and stood up where he had always stood when Sheelah unbuttoned him. He sat very still and stood very still, his grave little face intent with imagining. He was imagining how it would be when she did it. She would be right here, close—if he dared, he could put out his hand and smooth her. If he dared, he could take the pins out of her soft hair, and hide in it—

He meant to dare!

"Little silly," perhaps she would call him; perhaps she would remember to kiss him good-night. And afterwards, when the lark was over, it would stay on, singing in his heart. And he would lie in the dark and love Her.

For Her part, it was a busy day enough and did not lag. She did her shopping and called on a town friend or two. In the late afternoon she ran in to several art-stores where pictures were on exhibition. It was at the last of these places that she chanced to meet a woman who was a neighbor of hers in the suburbs.

"Why, Mrs. Cody!" the neighbor cried. "How delightful! You've come in to see Irving, too?"

"No," with distinct regret answered Murray's mother, "but I wish I had! I'm only in for a little shopping."

"Not going to stay! Why, it will be wicked to go back to-night—unless, of course, you've seen him in Robespierre."

"I haven't. Cicely Howe has been teasing me to stop over and go with her. It's a 'sure-enough' temptation, as Fred says. Fred's away, so that part's all right. Of course there's Murray, but there's also Sheelah—" She was talking more to herself now than to the neighbor. The temptation had taken a sudden and striking hold upon her. It was the chance of a lifetime. She really ought—

"I guess you'll stop over!" laughed the neighbor. "I know the signs."

"I'll telephone to Sheelah," Murray's mother decided, aloud, "then I'll run along back to Cicely's. I've always wanted to see Irving in that play."

But it was seven o'clock before she telephoned. She was to have been at home at half-past seven.

"That you, Sheelah? I'm not coming out to-night—not until morning. I'm going to the theatre. Tell Murray I'll bring him a present. Put an extra blanket over him if it comes up chilly."

She did not hang up the receiver at once, holding it absently at her ear while she considered if she ought to say anything else to Sheelah. Hence she heard distinctly an indignant exclamation.

"Will you hear that, now! An' the boy that certain! 'She's promised,' he says, an' he'll kape on 'She's-promising' for all o' me, for it's not tell him I will! He can go to slape in his poor little boots, expectin' her to kape her promise!"

The woman with the receiver at her ear uttered a low exclamation. She had not forgotten the Promise, but it had not impressed her as anything vital. She had given it merely to comfort Little Silly when he cried. That he would regard it as sacred—that it was sacred—came to her now with the forcible impact of a blow. And, oddly enough, close upon its heels came a remembrance picture—of a tiny child playing with his soldiers on the floor. The sunlight lay over him—she could see it on his little hair and face. She could hear him talking to the

"Captain soldier." She had at the time called it a sermon, with a text, and laughed at the child who preached it. She was not laughing now.

"Lissen, Cappen Sojer, an' I'll teach you a p'omise. A p'omise—a p'omise—why, when anybody p'omises, they do it!"

Queer how plainly she could hear Little Silly say that and could see him sitting in the sun! Just the little white dress he had on—tucks in it and a dainty edging of lace! She had recognized Sheelah's maxims and laughed. Sheelah was stuffing the child with notions.

"If anybody p'omises, they do it." It seemed to come to her over the wire in a baby's voice and to strike against her heart. This mother of a little son stood suddenly self-convicted of a crime—the crime of faithlessness. It was not, she realized with a sharp stab of pain, faith in her the little child at the other end of the line was exercising, but faith in the Promise. He would keep on "She-promising" till he fell asleep in his poor little boots—

"Oh!" breathed in acute distress the mother of a little son. For all unexpectedly, suddenly, her house built of cards of carelessness, flippancy, thoughtlessness, had fallen round her. She struggled among the flimsy ruins.

Then came a panic of hurry. She must go home at once, without a moment's delay. A little son was waiting for her to come and put him to bed. She had promised; he was waiting. They were to have a regular little lark—that she remembered, too, with distinctness. She was almost as uncertain as Murray had been of the meaning of a "lark"; she had used the word, as she had used so many other words to the child, heedlessly. She had even and odd, uncertain little feeling as to what it meant to put a little son to bed, for she had never unlaced or unbuttoned one. She had never wanted to until now. But now—she could hardly wait to get home to do it. Little Silly was growing up—the bare brown space between the puffs of his little trousers and the top rims of his little socks were widening. She must hurry, hurry! What if he grew up before she got there! What if she never had a chance to put a little son to bed! She had lost so many chances; this one that was left had suddenly sprung into prominence and immense value. With the shock of her awakening upon her she felt like one partially paralyzed, but with the need upon her to rise and walk—to run.

She started at once, scarcely allowing herself time to explain to her friend. She would listen to no urgings at all.

"I've got to go, Cicely—I've promised my little son," was all she took time to say; and the friend, knowing of the telephone message, supposed it had been a telephone promise.

At the station they told her there was another train at seven-thirty, and she walked about uneasily until it came. Walking about seemed to hurry it along the rails to her.

Another woman waited and walked with her. Another mother of little sons, she decided whimsically, reading it in the sweet, quiet face. The other woman was in widow's black, and she thought how merciful it was that there should be a little son left her. She yielded to an inclination to speak.

"The train is late," she said. "It must be."

"No." The other woman glanced backward at the station clock. "It's we who are early."

"And in a hurry," laughed Murray's mother, in the relief of speech. "I've got to get home to put my little son to bed! I don't suppose you are going home for that?"

The sweet face for an instant lost its quietness. Something like a spasm of mortal pain crossed it and twisted it. The woman walked away abruptly, but came back. "I've been home and—put him to bed," she said, slowly—"in his last little bed."

Then Murray's mother found herself hurrying feverishly into a car, her face feeling wet and queer. She was crying.

"Oh, the poor woman!" she thought, "the poor woman! And I'm going home to a little live one. I can cover him up and tuck him in! I can kiss his little, solemn face and his little, brown knees. Why haven't I ever kissed his knees before? If I could only hurry! Will this car ever start?" She put her head out of the window. An oily personage in jumpers was passing.

"Why don't we start?" she said.

"Hot box," the oily person replied, laconically.

The delay was considerable to a mother going home to put her little child to bed. It seemed to this mother interminable. When at length she felt a welcome jar and lurch her patience was threadbare. She sat bolt upright, as if by so doing she were helping things along.

It was an express and leaped ahead splendidly, catching up with itself. Her thoughts leaped ahead with it. No, no, he would not be in bed. Sheelah was not going to tell him, so he would insist upon waiting up. But she might find him asleep in his poor little boots! She caught her breath in half a sob, half tender laugh. Little Silly!

But if an express, why this stop? They were slowing up. It was not time to get to the home station; there were no lights. Murray's mother waylaid a passing brakeman.

"What is it? What is it?"

"All right, all right! Don't be scairt, lady! Wreck ahead somewheres—freight-train. We got to wait till they clear the track."

But the misery of waiting! He might get tired of waiting, or Sheelah might tell him his mother was not coming out to-night; he might go to bed, with his poor little faith in the Promise wrecked, like the freight on there in the dark. She could not sit still and bear the thought; it was not much easier pacing the aisle. She felt a wild inclination to get off the train and walk home.

At the home station, when at last she reached it, she took a carriage. "Drive fast!" she said, peremptorily. "I'll pay you double fare."

The houses they rattle past were ablaze with light down-stairs, not up-stairs where little sons would be going to bed. All the little sons had gone to bed.

They stopped with a terrific lurch. It threw her on to the seat ahead.

"This is not the place," she cried, sharply, after a glance without.

"No'm; we're stopping fer recreation," drawled sarcastically the unseen driver. He appeared to be assisting the horse to lie down. She stumbled to the ground and demanded things.

"Yer'll have to ax this here four-legged party what's doin'. I didn't stop—I kep' right on goin'. He laid down on his job, that's all, marm. I'll get him up, come Chris'mas. Now then, yer ole fool!"

There was no patience left in the "fare" standing there beside the plunging beast. She fumbled in her purse, found something, dropped it somewhere, and hurried away down the street. She did not walk home, because she ran. It was well the streets were quiet ones.

"Has he gone to bed?" she came panting in upon drowsy Sheelah, startling that phlegmatic person out of an honest Irish dream.

"Murray—Little Silly—has he gone to bed? Oh no!" for she saw him then, an inert little heap at Sheelah's feet. She gathered him up in her arms.

"I won't! I won't go, Sheelah! I'm waiting. She promis—" in drowsy murmur.

"She's here—she's come, Murray! Mamma's come home to put you to bed—Little Silly, open your eyes and see mamma!"

And he opened them and saw the love in her eyes before he saw her. Sleep took instant wings. He sprang up.

"I knew you'd come! I told Sheelah! When anybody promises, they— Come on quick up-stairs! I can unlace myself, but I'd rather—"

"Yes, yes!" she sobbed.

"And we'll have a lark, won't we? You said a lark; but not the reg'larest kind—I don't suppose we could have the reg'larest kind?"

"Yes—yes!"

"Oh!—why!" His eyes shone. He put up his hand, then drew it shyly back. If she would only take out the pins herself—if he only dared to—

"What is it, Little Silly—darling?" They were up in his room. She had her cheek against his little, bare, brown knees. It brought her soft, gold-colored hair so near—if he only dared—

"What is it you'd like, little son?" And he took courage. She had never called him Little Son before. It made him brave enough.

"I thought—the reg'larest kind—your hair—if you'd let it tumble all down, I'd—hide in it," he breathed, his knees against her cheek trembling like little frightened things.

It fell about him in a soft shower and he hid in it and laughed. Sheelah heard them laughing together.

Chapter IX

The Little Lover

"I wish I knew for very certain," the Little Lover murmured, wistfully. The licorice-stick was so shiny and black, and he had laid his tongue on it one sweet instant, so he knew just how good it tasted. If he only knew for very certain—of course there was a chance that She did not love licorice sticks. It would be a regular pity to waste it. Still, how could anybody not love 'em—

"'Course She does!" exclaimed the Little Lover, with sudden conviction, and the struggle was ended. It had only been a question of Her liking or not liking. That decided, there was no further hesitation. He held up the licorice-stick and traced a wavery little line round it with his finger-nail. The line was pretty near one of its ends—the end towards the Little Lover's mouth.

"I'll suck as far down as that, just 'xactly," he said; "then I'll put it away in the Treasury Box."

He sat down in his little rocker and gave himself up to the moment's bliss, first applying his lips with careful exactitude to the dividing-line between Her licorice stick and his.

The moment of bliss ended, the Little Lover got out the Treasury Box and added the moist, shortened licorice-stick to the other treasures in it. There were many of them,—an odd assortment that would have made any one else smile. But the Little Lover was not smiling. His small face was grave first, then illumined with the light of willing sacrifice. The treasures were all so beautiful! She would be so pleased,—my, my, how please She would be! Of course She would like the big golden alley the best,—the very best. But the singing-top was only a tiny little way behind in its power to charm. Perhaps She had never seen a singing-top—think o' that! Perhaps She had never had a great golden alley, or a corkscrew jack-knife, or a canary-bird whistle, or a red and white "Kandy Kiss,"—or a licorice-stick! Think o' that—think of how pleased She would be!

"'Course She will," laughed the Little Lover in his delight. If he only dared to give Her the Treasury Box! If he only knew how! If there was somebody he could ask,—but the housekeeper was too old, and Uncle Larry would laugh. There was nobody.

The waiting wouldn't be so bad if it wasn't for the red-cheeked pear in the Treasury Box, and the softest apple. They made it a little dang'rous to wait.

It had not been very long that he had loved Her. The first Sunday that She smiled at him across the aisle was the beginning. He had not gone to sleep that Sunday, nor since, on any of the smiling Sundays. He had not wanted to. It had been rest enough to sit and watch Her from the safe shelter of the housekeeper's silken cloak. Her clear, fresh profile, Her pretty hair, Her ear, Her throat—he liked to watch them all. It was rest enough,—as if, after that, he could have gone to sleep!

She was very tall, but he liked her better for that. He meant to be tall some day. Just now he did not reach— But he did not wish to think of that. It troubled him to remember that Sunday that he had measured himself secretly beside Her, as the people walked out of church. It made him blush to think how very little way he had "reached." He had never told any one, but then he never told any one anything. Not having any mother, and your father being away all the time, and the housekeeper being old, and your uncle Larry always laughing, made it diff'rent 'bout telling things. Of course if you had 'em—mothers, and fathers that stayed at home, and uncles that didn't laugh,—but you didn't. So you 'cided it was better not to tell things.

One Sunday the Little Lover thought he detected Uncle Larry watching Her too. But he was never quite certain sure. Anyway, when She had turned Her beautiful head and smiled across the aisle, it had been at him. The Little Lover was "certain sure" of that! In his shy little way he had smiled back at Her and nodded. The warmth had kept on in his heart all day. That was the day before he found out the Important Thing.

Out in the front hall after supper he came upon a beautiful, tantalizing smell that he failed for some time to locate. He went about with his little nose up-tilted, in a persistent search. It was such a beautiful smell!—not powerful and oversweet, but faint and wonderful. The little nose searched on patiently till it found it. There was a long box on the hall-table and the beautiful smell came out under the lid and met the little, up-tilted nose half-way.

"I've found it! It's inside o' that box!" the Little Lover cried in triumph. "Now I guess I better see what it looks like. Oh! why, it's posies!" For there, in moist tissue wrappings, lay a cluster of marvellous pale roses, breathing out their subtle sweetness into the little face above them.

"Why, I didn't know that was the way a beautiful smell looked! I—it's very nice, isn't it? If it's Uncle Larry's, I'm goin' to ask him— Oh, Uncle Larry, can I have it? Can I? I want to put it in Her—" But he caught himself up before he got quite to "Treasury Box." He could not tell Uncle Larry about that.

The tall figure coming down the hall quickened its steps to a leap towards the opened box on the table. Uncle Larry's face was flushed, but he laughed—he always laughed.

"You little 'thafe o' the wurruld'!" he called out. "What are you doing with my roses?"

"I want 'em—please," persisted the child, eagerly, thinking of the Treasury Box and Her.

"Oh, you do, do you? But they're not for the likes o' you."

Sudden inspiration came to the Little Lover. If this was a Treasury Box,—if he were right on the edge of finding out how you gave one—

"Is—is it for a She?" he asked, breathless with interest.

"A—'She'?" laughed Uncle Larry, but something as faint and tender as the beautiful smell was creeping into his face. "Yes, it is for a She, Reggie,—the most beautiful She in the world," he added, gently. He was wrapping the beautiful smell again in the tissue wrappings.

Then it was a Treasury Box. Then you did the treasures up that way, in thin, rattly paper like that. Then what did you do? But he would find out.

"Oh, I didn't know," he murmured. "I didn't know that was the way! Do you send it by the 'spressman, then, Uncle Larry,—to—to Her, you know? With Her name on?"

Uncle Larry was getting into his overcoat. He laughed. The tender light that had been for an instant in his face he had put away again out of sight.

"No; I'm my own ''spressman.' You've got some things to learn, Reg, before you grow up."

"I'd ravver learn 'em now. Tell me 'em! Tell what you do then."

The old mocking light was back in Uncle Larry's eyes. This small chap with the earnest little face was good as a play.

"'Then'? Then, sure, I go to the door and ring the bell. Then I kneel on one knee like this, and hold out the box—"

"The Treasury Box—yes, go on."

"—Like this. And I say, 'Fair One, accept this humble offering, I beseech thee'—"

"Accept this hum-bul offering, I—I beseech thee"—the Little Lover was saying it over and over to himself. It was a little hard, on account o' the queer words in it. He was still saying it after Uncle Larry had gone. His small round face was intent and serious. When he had learned the words, he practised getting down on one knee and holding out an imaginary Treasury Box. That was easier than the queer words, but it made you feel funnier somewhere in your inside. You wanted to cry, and you were a little afraid somebody else would want to laugh.

The next afternoon the Little Lover carried his Treasury Box to Her. He had wrapped all the little treasures carefully in tissue like Uncle Larry's roses. But there was no beautiful smell creeping out;—there was something a little like a smell, but not a beautiful one. The Little Lover felt sorry for that.

She came to the door. It was a little discomposing on account of there being so little time to get your breath in. I-it made you feel funny.

But the Little Lover acted well his part. With a little gasp that was like a sob he sank on one knee and held up the Treasury Box to Her.

"Fair One," he quivered, softly, "accept this—offspring—no, I mean this hum-bul offspring, I—I—oh, I mean please!"

She stooped to the level of his little, solemn face. Then suddenly She lifted him, Treasury Box and all, and bore him into a great, bright room.

"Why, Reggie!—you are Reggie, aren't you? You're the little boy that smiles at me across the aisle in church? I thought so! Well, I am so glad you have come to see me. And to think you have brought me a present, too—"

"I be-seech thee!" quivered the Little Lover, suddenly remembering the queer words that had eluded him before. He drew a long, happy breath. It was over now. She had the Treasury Box in her hand. She would open it by-and-by and find the golden alley and the singing-top and the licorice-stick. He wished he dared tell Her to open it soon on account o' the softest apple and the red-cheeked pear. Perhaps he would dare to after a little while. It was so much easier, so far, than he had expected.

She talked to him in Her beautiful, low-toned voice, and by-and-by She sat down to the piano and sang to him. That was the ve-ry best. He curled up on the sofa and listened, watching Her clear profile and Her hair and Her pretty moving fingers, in his Little Lover way. She looked so beautiful!—it made you want to put your cheek against Her sleeve and rub it very softly back and forth, back and forth, over and over again. If you only dared to!

So he was very happy until he smelled the beautiful smell again. All at once it crept to him across the room. He recognized it instantly as the same one that had crept out from under the lid of Uncle Larry's box. It was there, in the great, bright room! He slid to his feet and went about tracing it with his little up-tilted nose. It led him across to Her, and then he saw Uncle Larry's roses on Her breast. He uttered the softest little cry of pain—so soft She did not hear it in Her song—and crept back to his seat. He had had his first wound. He was only six, but at six it hurts.

It was Uncle Larry's roses She wore on Her dress—then it was roses She liked, not licorice-sticks and golden alleys. Then it was Uncle Larry's roses,—then She must like Uncle Larry. Then—oh, then, She would never like him! Perhaps it was Uncle Larry She had smiled at all the time, across the aisle. Uncle Larry "reached" so far! He wouldn't have to grow.

"She b'longs to Uncle Larry, an' I wanted Her to b'long to me. Nobody else does—I wouldn't have needed anybody else to, if She had. All I needed to b'long was Her. I wanted Her! I—I love Her. She isn't Uncle Larry's—she's mine!—She's mine!" The thoughts of the Little Lover surged on turbulently, while the beautiful low song went on. She was singing—She was singing to Uncle Larry. The song wasn't sweet and soft and tender for him. It was sweet and soft and tender for Uncle Larry.

"I hate Uncle Larry!" cried out the Little Lover, but She did not hear. She was lost in the tender depths of the song. It was very late in the afternoon and a still darkness was creeping into the big, bright room. The Little Lover nestled among the cushions of the sofa, spent with excitement and loss, and that new, dread feeling that made him hate Uncle Larry. He did not know its name, and it was better so. But he knew the pain of it.

"Why, Reggie! Why, you poor little man, you're asleep! And I have been sitting there singing all this time! And it grew quite dark, didn't it? Oh, poor little man, poor little man, I had forgotten you were here! I'm glad you can't hear me say it!"

Yes, it was better. But he would have like to feel Her cool cheek against his cheek; he would have felt a little relief in his desolate, bitter heart if he could see how gentle Her face was and the beautiful look there was in Her soft eyes. But perhaps—if She was not looking at him—if it was at Uncle Larry— No, no, Little Lover; it is better to sleep on and not to know.

It was Uncle Larry who carried him home, asleep still, and laid him gently on his own little bed. Uncle Larry's bearded face was shining in the dark room like a star. The tumult of joy in the man's heart clamored for utterance. Uncle Larry felt the need of telling some one. So, because he could not help it, he leaned down and shook the Little Lover gently.

"You little foolish chap, do you know what you have lost? You were right there—you might have heard Her when She said it! You might have peeped between your fingers and seen Her face—angels in Heaven! Her face!—with the love-light in it. You poor little chap! you poor little chap! You were right there all the time and you didn't know. And you don't know now when I tell you I'm the happiest man alive! You lie there like a little log. Well, sleep away, little chap. What does it matter to you?"

It was the Little Lover's own guardian-angel who kept him from waking up, but Uncle Larry did not know. He took off the small, dusty shoes and loosened the little clothes, with a strange new tenderness in his big fingers. The familiar little figure seemed to have put on a certain sacredness for having lain on Her cushions and been touched by Her hands. And She had kissed the little chap. Uncle Larry stooped and found the place with his lips.

The visit seemed like a dream to the Little Lover, next morning. How could it have been real when he could not remember coming home at all? Hehadn't come home,—so of course he had never gone. It was a dream,—still—where was the Treasury Box?

"I wish I knew for very certain," the Little Lover mused. "I could ask Uncle Larry, but I hate Uncle Larry—" Oh! Then it wasn't a dream. It was true. It all came back. The Little Lover remembered why he hated Uncle Larry. He remembered it all. Lying there in his little bed he smelt the beautiful smell again and followed it up to the roses on Her dress. They were Uncle Larry's roses, so he hated Uncle Larry. He always would. He did not hate Her, but he would never go to see Her again. He would never nod or smile at Her again in church. He would never be happy again.

Perhaps She would send back the Treasury Box;—the Little Lover had heard once that people sent back things when it was all over. It was all over now. He was only six, but the pain in his heart was so big that he did not think to wish She would send back the Treasury Box soon, on account of the softest apple.

The days went by until they made a month,—two months,—half a year. The pain in the Little Lover's heart softened to a dreary loneliness, but that stayed on. He had always been a lonely little chap, but not like this. He had never had a mother, and his father had nearly always been away. But this was different. Now he had nobody to love, and he hated Uncle Larry.

That was before the Wonderful Thing happened. One day Uncle Larry brought Her home. He said She was his wife. That was the Wonderful Thing.

The Little Lover ran away and hid. They could not find him for a long time. It was She who found him.

"Why, Reggie! Why, poor little man! Look up. What is it, dear? Reggie, you are crying!"

He did not care. He wanted to cry. But he let Her take him into Her arms.

"I wanted to do it!" he sobbed, desolately, his secret out at last.

"Do it? Do what, Reggie?"

"M-marry you. I was goin' to do it. H-He hadn't any right to! I hate him—I hate him!"

A minute there was silence, except for the soft creak of Her dress as She rocked him. Then She lifted his wet little face to Hers.

"Reggie," She whispered, "how would a mother do?"

He nestled his cheek against Her sleeve and rubbed it back and forth, back and forth, while he thought. A mother—then there would be no more loneliness. Then there would be a place to cuddle in, and somebody to tell things to. "I'd ravver a mother," the Little Lover said.

Chapter X

The Child

The Child had it all reasoned out in her own way. It was only lately she had got to the end of her reasoning and settled down. At first it had not been very satisfactory, but she had gradually, with a child's optimism, evolved from the dreary little maze a certain degree of content.

She had only one confidant. The Child had always lived a rather proscribed, uneventful little life, with pitifully few intimates,—none of her own age. The Child was eight.

The confidant, oddly, was a picture in the silent, awe-inspiring company-room. It represented a lady with a beautiful face, and a baby in her arms. The Child had never heard it called a Madonna, but it was because of that picture that she was never afraid in the company-room. Going in and out so often to confide things to the Lady had bred a familiarity with the silent place that came to amount in the end to friendliness. The Lady was always there, smiling gently at the Child, and so the other things did not matter—the silence and the awe-inspiringness.

The Child told the Lady everything, standing down under the picture and looking up at it adoringly. She was explaining her conclusions concerning the Greatest Thing of All now.

"I didn't tell you before," she said. "I wanted to get it reasoned out. If," rather wistfully, "you were a—a flesh-and-bloody lady, you could tell me if I haven't got it right. But I think I have.

"You see, there are a great many kinds of fathers and mothers, but I'm only talking of my kind. I'm going to love my father one day and my mother the next. Like this: my mother Monday, my father Tuesday, mother Wednesday, father Thursday—right along. Of course you can't divide seven days even, but I'm going to love them both on Sundays. Just one day in the week I don't think it will do any harm, do you?— Oh, you darling Lady, I wish you could shake your head or bow it! I'm only eight, you see, and eight isn't a very reasonable age. But I couldn't think of any better way."

The Child's eyes riveted to the beautiful face almost saw it nod a little.

"I haven't decided 'xactly, but perhaps I shall love my mother Sunday mornings and my father Sunday afternoons. If—if it seems best to. I'll let you know." She stopped talking and thought a minute in her serious little way. She was considering whether to say the next thing or not. Even to the Lady she had never said why-things about her father and mother. If the Lady knew—and she had lived so long in the company-room, it seemed as if she must,—then there was no need of explaining. And if she didn't know—suddenly the Child, with a throb of pride, hoped that the Lady did not know. But perhaps some slight explanation was necessary.

"Of course," the Child burst out, hurriedly, her cheeks aflame,—"of course it would be nice to love both of 'em the same day, but—but they're not that kind of a father and mother. I've thought it all over and made the reasonablest plan I know how to. I'm going to begin to-morrow—to-morrow is Tuesday, my father's day."

It was cold in the company-room, and any moment Marie might come and take her away. She was always a little pressed for time.

"I must be going," she said, "or Marie will come. Good-bye. Give my love to the baby." She always sent her love to the baby in the beautiful Lady's arms.

The Child's home, though luxurious, had to her the effect of being a double tenement. An invisible partition divided her father's side from her mother's; her own little white room, with Marie's alcove, seemed to be across the dividing line, part on one side, part on the other. She could remember when there had not been any invisible partition, but the intensity of her little mental life since there had been one had dimmed the beautiful remembrance. It seemed to her now as a pleasant dream that she longed to dream again.

The next day the Child loved her father, for it was Tuesday. She went about it in her thorough, conscientious little way. She had made out a little programme. At the top of the sheet, in her clear, upright hand, was, "Ways to Love My farther." And after that:

- "1. Bringing in his newspaper.
- "2. Kissing Him goodmorning.
- "3. Rangeing his studdy table.
- "4. Putting flours on "   "
- "5. Takeing up His male.
- "6. Reeching up to rub My cheak against his cheak.
- "7. Lerning to read so I can read His Books."

There were many other items. The Child had used three pages for her programme. The last two lines read:

- "Praing for Him.
- "Kissing Him goodnight."

The Wednesday programme was almost identical with this one, with the exception of "my mother" instead of "my farther." For the Child did not wish to be partial. She had always had a secret notion that it would be a little easier to read her mother's books, but she meant to read just as many of her "farther's."

During the morning she went in to the Lady and reported progress so far. Her cheeks were a delicate pink with excitement, and she panted a little when she spoke.

"I'm getting along splendidly," she said, smiling up at the beautiful face. "Perhaps—of course I can't tell for sure, but I'm not certain but that he will like it after he gets used to it. You have to get used to things. He liked the flowers, and when I rubbed my cheek 'gainst his, and when I kissed him. How I know he did is because he smiled—I wish my father would smile all the time."

The Child did not leave the room when she had finished her report, but fidgeted about the great silent place uncertainly. She turned back by-and-by to the Lady.

"There's something I wish you could tell me," she said, with her wistful little face uplifted. "It's if you think it would be polite to ask my father to put me to bed instead of Marie—just unbutton me, you know, and pray me. I was going to ask my mother to-morrow night if my father did to-night. I thought—I thought"—the Child hesitated for adequate words—"it would be the lovingest way to love him, for you feel a little intimater with persons when they put you to bed. Sometimes I feel that way with Marie—a very little. I wish you could nod your head if you thought it would be polite."

The Child's eyes, fastened upon the picture, were intently serious. And again the Lady seemed to nod.

"Oh, you're nodding, yes!—I b'lieve you're nodding yes! Thank you ve-ry much—now I shall ask him to. Good-bye. Give my love to the baby." And the little figure moved away sedately.

To ask him in the manner of a formal invitation with "yours very truly" in it appeared to the Child upon thoughtful deliberation to be the best way. She did not feel very intimate yet with her father, but of course it might be different after he unbuttoned her and prayed her.

Hence the formal invitation:

"Dear farther you are respectably invited to put yore little girl to bed tonite at ½ past 7. Yores very truely

Elizabeth.

"R s v p.

P.s. the little girl is me."

It was all original except the "R s v p" and the fraction. The Child had asked Marie how to write "half," and the other she had found in the corner of one of her mother's formal invitations. She did not know what the four letters meant, but they made the invitation look nicer, and she could make lovely capital "R's."

At lunch-time the Child stole up-stairs and deposited her little folded note on top of her father's manuscript. Her heart beat strangely fast as she did it. She had still a lurking fear that it might not be polite.

On the way back she hurried into the company-room, up to the Lady. "I've done it!" she reported, breathlessly. "I hope it was polite—oh, I hope he will!"

The Child's father ate his lunch silently and a little hastily, as if to get it over. On the opposite side of the table the Child's mother ate hers silently and a little hastily. It was the usual way of their meals. The few casual things they said had to do with the weather or the salad. Then it was over and they separated, each to his own side of the divided house.

The father took up his pen to write—it seemed all there was left to do now. But the tiny folded note arrested his hand, and he stared in amazement. The Child had inadvertently set her seal upon it in the form of a little finger-print. So he knew it was hers. The first shock of hope it had awakened subsided into mere curiosity. But when he opened it, when he read it—

He sat a long time very still indeed—so still he could hear the rustle of manuscript pages in the other writing-room across the hall. Perhaps he sat there nearly all the afternoon, for the shadows lengthened before he seemed to move.

In the rush of thoughts that came to him two stood out most clearly—the memory of an awful day, when he had seemed to die a thousand deaths, and only come to life when a white-capped nurse came smiling to him and said, "It is a little girl," and the memory of a day two years ago, when a man and a woman had faced each other and said, "We will try to bear it for the child."

The Child found her answer lying on her plate at nursery tea. Marie, who was bustling about the room getting things orderly for the night, heard a little gasp and turned in alarm. The Child was spelling out her letter with a radiant face that belied the gasp. There was something in the lonely little figure's eagerness that appealed even to the unemotional maid, and for a moment there was likelihood of a strange thing happening. But the crisis was quickly over, and Marie, with the kiss unkissed on her lips, went on with her work. Emotions were rare with Marie.

"'Dear Little Girl, Who Is You,'" spelled the Child, in a soft ecstasy, yet not without dread of what might come, supposing he thought she had been impo—

"'Dear Little Girl, Who Is You,'" she hurriedly began again, "'your farther will be happy to accept your kind invitation for ½ past 7 this evening. Will you please call for him, as he is a little—b-a-s-h-f-u-l'—Marie, what does b-a-s-h-f-u-l spell?" shrilled the eager voice. It was a new word.

Marie came over to the Child's chair. "How can I tell without I see it?" she said. But the Child drew away gently.

"This is a very intimate letter—you'll have to 'xcuse seeing it. Never mind, anyway, thank you,—I can guess it." And she guessed that it spelled the way she would feel when she called for her father at half-past seven, for the Child was a little bashful, too. She told the Lady so.

"I don't dread it; I just wish it was over," she explained. "It makes me feel a little queer, you see. Probably you wouldn't feel that way if you was better acquainted with a person. Fathers and mothers are kind of strangers."

She was ready at seven o'clock, and sat, a little patient statue, watching the nursery clock. Marie, who had planned to go out and had intended setting the hands of the clock ahead a little, was unwarrantably angry with the Child for sitting there so persistently. "Come," she said, impatiently; "I've got your night-gown ready. This clock's too slow."

"Truly, is it?" the Child questioned, anxiously. "Slow means it's 'most half-past, doesn't it? Then I ought to be going!"

"Yes,—come along;" but Marie meant to bed, and the Child was already on her way to her father. She hurried back on second thought to explain to Marie.

"I've engaged somebody—there's somebody else going to put me to bed to-night. You needn't wait, Marie," she said, her voice oddly subdued and like some other little girl's voice in her repressed excitement.

He was waiting for her. He had been ready since half-past six o'clock. Without a word—with only an odd little smile that set the Child at ease—he took her hand and went back with her. The door of the other writing-room was ajar, and they caught a glimpse as they went by of a slender, stooping figure. It did not turn.

"This is my room," the Child introduced, gayly. The worst was over now and all the rest was best. "You've never been in my room before, have you? This is where I keep my clothes, and this is my undressing-chair. This is where Marie sits—you're Marie to-night!" The Child's voice rang out in sudden, sweet laughter. It was such a funny idea! She was not a laughing Child, and the little, rippling sound had the effect of escaping from imprisonment and exulting at its freedom.

"You never unbuttoned a little girl before, did you? I'll have to learn you."

"Teach you," he corrected, gently.

"Marie says learn you. But of course I'll say 'teach' if you like it better," with the ready courtesy of a hostess. "You begin with my feet and go backwards!" Again the escaped laughter. The Child was happy.

Down the hall where the slender figure stooped above the delicately written pages the little laugh travelled again and again. By-and-by another laugh, deep and rich, came hand in hand with it. Then the figure straightened tensely, for this new laugh was rarer even than the Child's. Two years—two years and more since she had heard this one.

"Now it is time to pray me," the Child said, dropping into sudden solemnity. "Marie lets me kneel to her—" hesitating questioningly. Then: "It's pleasanter to kneel to somebody—"

"Kneel to me," he whispered. His face grew a little white, and his hand, when he caressed lightly the frolic-rumpled little head, was not steady. The stone mask of the man dropped off completely, and underneath was tenderness and pain and love.

"Now I lame me down to sleep—no, I want to say another one to-night, Lord God, if Thee please. This is a very particular night, because my father is in it. Bless my father, Lord God, oh, bless my father! This is his day. I've loved him all day, and I'm going to again day after to-morrow. But to-morrow I must love my mother. It would be easier to love them both forever and ever, Amen."

The Child slipped into bed and slept happily, but the man who was father of the Child had new thoughts to think, and it took time. He found he had not thought nearly all of them in his afternoon vigil. On his way back to his lonely study he walked a little slower past the other lonely study. The stooping of the slender figure newly troubled him.

The plan worked satisfactorily to the Child, though there was always the danger of getting the days mixed. The first mother-day had been as "intimate" and delightful as the first father-one. They followed each other intimately and delightfully in a long succession. Marie found her perfunctory services less and less in requisition, and her dazed comprehension of things was divided equally with her self-gratulation. Life in this new and unexpected condition of affairs was easier to Marie.

"I'm having a beautiful time," the Child one day reported to the Lady, "only sometimes I get a little dizzy trying to remember which is which. My father is which to-day." And it was at that bedtime, after an unusually active day, that the Child fell asleep at her prayer. Her rumpled head sagged more and more on her delicate neck, till it rested sidewise on the supporting knees, and the Child was asleep.

There was a slight stir in the doorway.

"'Sh! don't move—sit perfectly still!" came in a whisper as a slender figure moved forward softly into the room.

"Richard, don't move! The poor little tired thing—do you think you could slip out without moving while I hold up her head—oh, I mean withoutjoggling? Now—oh, mamma's little tired baby! There, there!—'Sh! Now you hold her head and let me sit down—now put her here in my arms, Richard."

The transfer was safely made. They faced each other, she with her baby, he standing looking down at them. Their eyes met steadily. The Child's regular breathing alone stirred the silence of the little white room. Then he stooped to kiss the Child's face as she stooped, and their kisses seemed to meet. She did not start away, but smiled instead.

"I want her every day, Richard!" she said.

"I want her every day, Mary!"

"Then there is only one way. Last night she prayed to have things changed round—"

"Yes, Polly?"

"We'll change things round, Dick."

The Child was smiling in her sleep as if she heard them.

Chapter XI

The Recompense

There were all kinds of words,—short ones and long ones. Some were very long. This one—we-ell, maybe it wasn't so long, for when you're nine you don't of course mind three-story words, and this one looked like a three-story one. But this one puzzled you the worst ever!

Morry spelled it through again, searching for light. But it was a very dark word. Rec-om-pense,—if it meant anything money-y, then they'd made a mistake, for of course you don't spell "pence" with an "s."

The dictionary was across the room, and you had to stand up to look up things in it,—Morry wished it was not so far away and that you could do it sitting down. He sank back wearily on his cushions and wished other things, too: That Ellen would come in, but that wasn't a very big wish, because Ellens aren't any good at looking up words. That dictionaries grew on your side o' the room,—that wish was a funny one! That Dadsy would come home—oh, oh, that Dadsy would come home!

With that wish, which was a very Big One indeed, came trooping back all Morry's Troubles. They stood round his easy-chair and pressed up close against him. He hugged the most intimate ones to his little, thin breast.

It was getting twilight in the great, beautiful room, and twilight was trouble-time. Morry had found that out long ago. It's when it's too dark to read and too light for Ellens to come and light the lamps that you say "Come in!" to your troubles. They're always there waiting.

If Dadsy hadn't gone away to do—that. If he'd just gone on reg'lar business, or on a hurry-trip across the ocean, or something like that. You could count the days and learn pieces to surprise him with when he got back, and keep saying, "Won't it be splendid!" But this time—well, this time it scared you to have Dadsy come home. And if you learned a hundred pieces you knew you'd never say 'em to him—now. And you kept saying, "Won't it be puffectly dreadful!"

"Won't you have the lamps lit, Master Morris?" It was Ellen's voice, but the Troubles were all talking at once, and much as ever he could hear it.

"I knew you weren't asleep because your chair creaked, so I says, 'I guess we'll light up,'—it's enough sight cheerier in the light"; and Ellen's thuddy steps came through the gloom and frightened away the Troubles.

"Thank you," Morry said, politely. It's easy enough to remember to be polite when you have so much time. "Now I'd like Jolly,—you guess he's got home now, don't you?"

Ellen's steps sounded a little thuddier as they tramped back down the hall. "It's a good thing there's going to be a Her here to send that common boy kiting!" she was thinking. Yet his patches were all Ellen—so far—had seen in Jolly to find fault with. Though, for that matter, in a house beautiful like this patches were, goodness knew, out of place enough!

"Hully Gee, ain't it nice an' light in here!" presently exclaimed a boy's voice from the doorway.

"Oh, I'm so glad you've come, Jolly! Come right in and take a chair,—take two chairs!" laughed Morry, in his excess of welcome. It was always great when Jolly came! He and the Troubles were not acquainted; they were never in the room at the same time.

Morry's admiration of this small bepatched, befreckled, besmiled being had begun with his legs, which was not strange, they were such puffectly straight, limber, splendid legs and could go—my! Legs like that were great!

But it was noticeable that the legs were in some curious manner telescoped up out of sight, once Jolly was seated. The phenomenon was of common occurrence,—they were always telescoped then. And nothing had ever been said between the two boys about legs. About arms, yes, and eyes, ears, noses,—never legs. If Morry understood the kind little device to save his feelings, an instinctive knowledge that any expression of gratitude would embarrass Jolly must have kept back his ready little thank you.

"Can you hunt up things?" demanded the small host with rather startling energy. He was commonly a quiet, self-contained host. "Because there's a word—"

But Jolly had caught up his cap, untelescoped the kind little legs, and was already at the door. Nothing pleased him more than a commission from the Little White Feller in the soft chair there.

"I'll go hunt,—where'd I be most likely to find him?"

The Little White Feller rarely laughed, but now—"You—you Jolly boy!" he choked, "you'll find him under a hay-stack fast aslee— No, no!" suddenly grave and solicitous of the other's feelings, "in the dictionary, I mean. Words, don't you know?"

"Oh, get out!" grinned the Jolly boy, in glee at having made the Little White Feller laugh out like that, reg'lar-built. "Hand him over, then, but you'll have to do the spellin'."

"Rec-om-pense,—p-e-n-s-e," Morry said, slowly, "I found it in a magazine,—there's the greatest lot o' words in magazines! Look up 'rec,' Jolly,—I mean, please."

Dictionaries are terrible books. Jolly had never dreamed there were so many words in the world,—pages and pages and pages of 'em! The prospect of ever finding one particular word was disheartening, but he plunged in sturdily, determination written on every freckle.

"Don't begin at the first page!" cried Morry, hastily. "Begin at R,—it's more than half-way through. R-e,—r-e-c,—that way."

Jolly turned over endless pages, trailed laboriously his little, blunt finger up and down endless columns, wet his lips with the red tip of his tongue endless times,—wished 'twas over. He had meant to begin at the beginning and keep on till he got to a w-r-e-c-k,—at Number Seven they spelled it that way. Hadn't he lost a mark for spelling it without a "w"? But of course if folks preferred the r kind—

"Hi!" the blunt finger leaped into space and waved triumphantly. "R-e-c-k,—I got him!"

"Not 'k,'—there isn't any 'k.' Go backwards till you drop it, Jolly,—you dropped it?"

Dictionaries are terrible,—still, leaving a letter off o' the end isn't as bad as off o' the front. Jolly retraced his steps patiently.

"I've dropped it," he announced in time.

Morry was breathing hard, too. Looking up words with other people's fore-fingers is pretty tough.

"Now, the second story,—'rec' is the first," he explained. "You must find 'rec-om' now, you know."

No, Jolly did not know, but he went back to the work undaunted. "We'll tree him," he said, cheerily, "but I think I could do it easier if I whistled"—

"Whistle," Morry said.

With more directions, more hard breathing, more wetting of lips and tireless trailing of small, blunt finger, and then—eureka! there you were! But eureka was not what Jolly said.

"Bully for us!" he shouted. He felt thrilly with pride of conquest. "It's easy enough finding things. What's the matter with dictionaries!"

"Now read what it means, Jolly,—I mean, please. Don't skip."

"'Rec-om-pense: An equi-va-lent received or re-turned for anything given, done, or suff-er-ed; comp-ens-a-tion.'"

"That all?—every speck?"

"Well, here's another one that says 'To make a-mends,' if you like that one any better. Sounds like praying."

"Oh," sighed Morry, "how I'd like to know what equi-valent means!" but he did not ask the other to look it up. He sank back on his pillows and reasoned things out for himself the best way he could. "To make amends" he felt sure meant to make up. To make up for something given or suffered,—perhaps that was what a Rec-om-pense was. For something given or suffered—like legs, maybe? Limp, no-good-legs that wouldn't go? Could there be a Rec-om-pense for those? Could anything ever "make up"?

"Supposing you hadn't any legs, Jolly,—that would go?" he said, aloud, with disquieting suddenness. Jolly started, but nodded comprehendingly. He had not had any legs for a good many minutes; the telescoping process is numbing in the extreme.

"Do you think anything could ever Rec-om-pense—make up, you know? Especially if you suffered? Please don't speak up quick,—think, Jolly."

"I'm a-thinkin'." Not to have 'em that would go,—not go! Never to kite after Dennis O'Toole's ice-wagon an' hang on behind,—nor see who'd get to the corner first,—nor stand on your head an' wave 'em—

"No, sirree!" ejaculated Jolly, with unction, "nothin'."

"Would ever make up, you mean?" Morry sighed. He had known all the time, of course what the answer would be.

"Yep,—nothin' could."

"I thought so. That's all,—I mean, thank you. Oh yes, there's one other thing,—I've been saving it up. Did you ever hear of a—of a step-mother, Jolly? I just thought I'd ask."

The result was surprising. The telescoped legs came to view jerkily, but with haste. Jolly stumbled to his feet.

"I better be a-goin'," he muttered, thinking of empty chip-baskets, empty water-pails, undone errands,—a switch on two nails behind the kitchen door.

"Oh, wait a minute,—did you ever hear of one, Jolly?"

"You bet," gloomily, "I got one."

"Oh!—oh, I didn't know. Then," rather timidly, "perhaps—I wish you'd tell me what they're like."

"Like nothin'! Nobody likes 'em," came with more gloom yet from the boy with legs.

"Oh!" It was almost a cry from the boy without. This was terrible. This was a great deal terribler than he had expected.

"Would one be angry if—if your legs wouldn't go? Would it make her very, do you think?"

Still thinking of empty things that ought to have been filled, Jolly nodded emphatically.

"Oh!" The terror grew.

"Then one—then she—wouldn't be—be glad to see anybody, I suppose, whose legs had never been?—wouldn't want to shake hands or anything, I suppose?—nor be in the same room?"

"Nope." One's legs may be kind even to the verge of agony, but how unkind one's tongue may be! Jolly's mind was busy with his own anticipated woes; he did not know he was unkind.

"That's all,—thank you, I mean," came wearily, hopelessly, from the pillows. But Morry called the other back before he got over the threshold. There was another thing upon which he craved enlightenment. It might possibly help out.

"Are they pretty, Jolly?" he asked, wistfully.

"Are who what?" repeated the boy on the threshold, puzzled. Guilt and apprehension dull one's wits.

"Step-ones,—mothers."

Pretty? When they were lean and sharp and shabby! When they kept switches on two nails behind the door,—when they wore ugly clothes pinned together! But Jolly's eye caught the wistfulness on Morry's little, peaked, white face, and a lie was born within him at the sight. In a flash he understood things. Pity came to the front and braced itself stalwartly.

"You bet they're pretty!" Jolly exclaimed, with splendid enthusiasm. "Prettier'n anythin'! You'd oughter see mine!" (Recording Angel, make a note of it, when you jot this down, that the little face across the room was intense with wistfulness, and Jolly was looking straight that way. And remember legs.)

When Ellen came in to put Morry to bed she found wet spots on his cushions, but she did not mention them. Ellens can be wise. She only handled the limp little figure rather more gently than usual, and said rather more cheery things, perhaps. Perhaps that was why the small fellow under her hands decided to appeal in his desperation to her. It was possible—things were always possible—that Ellen might know something of—of step-ones. For Morry was battling with the pitifully unsatisfactory information Jolly had given him before understanding had conceived the kind little lie. It was, of course,—Morry put it that way because "of course" sometimes comforts you,—of course just possible that Jolly's step-one might be different. Ellen might know of there being another kind.

So, under the skilful, gentle hands, the boy looked up and chanced it. "Ellen," he said— "Ellen, are they all that kind,—all of 'em? Jolly's kind, I mean? I thought poss'bly you might know one"—

"Heart alive!" breathed Ellen, in fear of his sanity. She felt his temples and his wrists and his limp little body. Was he going to be sick now, just as his father and She were coming home?—now, of all times! Which would be better to give him, quinine, or aconite and belladonna?

"Never mind," sighed Morry, hopelessly. Ellens—he might have known—were not made to tell you close things like that. They were made to undress you and give you doses and laugh and wheel your chair around. Jollys were better than Ellens, but they told you pretty hard things sometimes.

In bed he lay and thought out his little puzzles and steeled himself for what was to come. He pondered over the word Jolly had looked up in the dictionary for him. It was a puzzly word,—Rec-om-pense,—but he thought he understood it now. It meant something that made up to you for something you'd suffered,—"suffered," that was what it said. And Morry had suffered—oh, how! Could it be possible there was anything that would make up for little, limp, sorrowful legs that had never been?

With the fickleness of night-thoughts his musings flitted back to step-ones again. He shut his eyes and tried to imagine just the right kind of one,—the kind a boy would be glad to have come home with his Dadsy. It looked an easy thing to do, but there were limitations.

"If I'd ever had a real one, it would be easier," Morry thought wistfully. Of course, any amount easier! The mothers you read about and the Holy Ones you saw in pictures were not quite real enough. What you needed was to have had one of your own. Then,—Morry's eyes closed in a dizzy little vision of one of his own. One that would have dressed and undressed you instead of an Ellen,—that would have moved your chair about and beaten up the cushions,—one that maybe would have loved you, legs and all!

Why!—why, that was the kind of a step-one a boy'd like to have come home with his father! That was the very kind! While you'd been lying there thinking you couldn't imagine one, you'd imagined! And it was easy!

The step-one a boy would like to have come home with his father seemed to materialize out of the dim, soft haze from the shaded night-lamp,—seemed to creep out of the farther shadows and come and stand beside the bed, under the ring of light on the ceiling that made a halo for its head. The room seemed suddenly full of its gracious presence. It came smiling, as a boy would like it to come. And in a reg'lar mother-voice it began to speak. Morry lay as if in a wondrous dream and listened.

"Are you the dear little boy whose legs won't go?" He gasped a little, for he hadn't thought of there being a "dear." He had to swallow twice before he could answer. Then:—

"Oh yes'm, thank you," he managed to say. "They're under the bedclothes."

"Then I've come to the right place. Do you know—guess!—who I am?"

"Are—are you a step-one?" breathing hard.

"Why, you've guessed the first time!" the Gracious One laughed.

"Not—not the one, I s'pose?" It frightened him to say it. But the Gracious One laughed again.

"The one, yes, you Dear Little Boy Whose Legs Won't Go! I thought I heard you calling me, so I came. And I've brought you something."

To think of that!

"Guess, you Dear Little Boy! What would you like it to be?"

Oh, if he only dared! He swallowed to get up courage. Then he ventured timidly.

"A Rec-om-pense." It was out.

"Oh, you Guesser—you little Guesser! You've guessed the second time!"

Was that what it was like? Something you couldn't see at all, just feel,—that folded you in like a warm shawl,—that brushed your forehead, your cheek, your mouth,—that made you dizzy with happiness? You lay folded up in it and knew that it made up. Never mind about the sorrowful, limp legs under the bedclothes. They seemed so far away that you almost forgot about them. They might have been somebody else's, while you lay in the warm, sweet Rec-om-pense.

"Will—will it last?" he breathed.

"Always, Morry."

The Gracious Step-one knew his name!

"Then Jolly didn't know this kind,—we never s'posed there was a kind like this! Real Ones must be like this."

And while he lay in the warm shawl, in the soft haze of the night-lamp, he seemed to fall asleep, and, before he knew, it was morning. Ellen had come.

"Up with you, Master Morris! There's great doings to-day. Have you forgot who's coming?"

Ellens are stupid.

"She's come." But Ellen did not hear, and went on getting the bath ready. If she had heard, it would only have meant quinine or aconite and belladonna to drive away feverishness. For Ellens are very watchful.

"They'll be here most as soon as I can get you up 'n' dressed. I'm going to wheel you to the front winder—"

"No!" Morry cried, sharply; "I mean, thank you, no. I'd rather be by the back window where—where I can watch for Jolly." Homely, freckled, familiar Jolly,—he needed something freckled and homely and familiar. The old dread had come back in the wake of the beautiful dream,—for it had been a dream. Ellen had waked him up.

A boy would like to have his father come home in the sunshine, and the sun was shining. They would come walking up the path to the front-door through it,—with it warm and welcoming on their faces. But it would only be Dadsy and a step-one,—Jolly's kind, most likely. Jolly's kind was pretty,—she might be pretty. But she would not come smiling and creeping out of the dark with a halo over her head. That kind came in dreams.

Jolly's whistle was comforting to hear. Morry leaned out of his cushions to wave his hand. Jolly was going to school; when he came whistling back, she would be here. It would be all over.

Morry leaned back again and closed his eyes. He had a way of closing them when he did the hardest thinking,—and this was the very hardest. Sometimes he forgot to open them, and dropped asleep. Even in the morning one can be pretty tired.

"Is this the Dear Little Boy?"

He heard distinctly, but he did not open his eyes. He had learned that opening your eyes drives beautiful things away.

The dream had come back. If he kept perfectly still and didn't breathe, it might all begin again. He might feel—

He felt it. It folded him in like a warm shawl,—it brushed his forehead, his cheek, his lips,—it made him dizzy with happiness. He lay among his cushions, folded up in it. Oh, it made up,—it made up, just as it had in the other dream!

"You Dear Little Boy Whose Legs Won't Go!"—he did not catch anything but the first four words; he must have breathed and lost the rest. But the tone was all there. He wanted to ask her if she had brought the Rec-om-pense, but it was such a risk to speak. He thought if he kept on lying quite still he should find out. Perhaps in a minute—

"You think he will let me love him, Morris? Say you think he will!"

Morris was Dadsy's other name. Things were getting very strange.

"Because I must! Perhaps it will make up a very little if I fold him all up in my love."

"Fold him up"—that was what the warm shawl had done, and the name of the warm shawl had been Rec-om-pense. Was there another name to it?

Morry opened his eyes and gazed up wonderingly into the face of the step-one.—It was a Real One's face, and the other name was written on it.

"Why, it's Love!" breathed Morry. He felt a little dizzy, but he wanted to laugh, he was so happy. He wanted to tell her—he must.

"It makes up—oh yes, it makes up!" he cried, softly.

Milton Keynes UK
Ingram Content Group UK Ltd.
UKHW020843260624
444769UK00011B/455